"*Emergency Stopping and Other Stories* is a collection full, not of characters, but of people, people you'll recognize; everyday folk doing their best to get along, and Vande Zande knows them well. These good-hearted stories are a fine debut in what we can only hope is a long, long career."

—Pete Fromm, author of *As Cool as I Am* and *How All this Started.*

EMERGENCY STOPPING
&
OTHER STORIES

Jeff Vande Zande

Working Lives Stories
Bottom Dog Press
Huron, Ohio

Acknowledgments:

Cover art by Matthew Watt
Cover design by Larry Smith
Book layout by Jason Teply

The author would like to thank the editors of the following magazines and anthologies, in which some of these
stories first appeared.

"Calling" in *Passages North;*
"Downstream Water" in *Crab Creek Review;*
"Emergency Stopping" in *The MacGuffin;*
"From the Slightest Wings" in *Pemmican*
"Layoff" in *Our Working Lives: Short Stories of People and
Work*, an anthology from Bottom Dog Press;
"Reception" in *Midnight Mind;*
"Trainee" in *Controlled Burn.*

Thanks to the Ohio Arts Council
for their continued support.

Ohio Arts Council
A STATE AGENCY
THAT SUPPORTS PUBLIC
PROGRAMS IN THE ARTS

Table of Contents

Calling

Jeff Vande Zande

Danny dropped his card into the time clock and its metallic thud sounded like a deadbolt locking. While waiting for the supervisor to show him around, he recalled how only two weeks ago he had been fired from his job bagging groceries. He could still remember the sound the wheels of a shopping cart made as they rattled across the parking lot. He remembered, too, how he'd lost that job.

* * *

Pushing her cart, Danny followed Mrs. Hudgins out to her car. He knew the old woman as an acquaintance of his mother's.

"There's nobody at home to help me like this," she sighed as she watched him load the bags into her trunk.

He shrugged, opened the passenger door, and told her that he'd come help her for a while. After he brought everything into her kitchen, she mentioned a few other things he could do—changing chandelier bulbs, replacing batteries in smoke detectors, replacing a furnace filter, cleaning clogged gutters, replacing a broken lock on the back door. She was happy to tell him what to do and didn't seem to find it strange that a thirty-year-old man wearing a *Red Owl* apron was running around her home doing odd jobs. After two hours, she pushed up to her tiptoes and kissed him on the cheek. "Bless you," she said.

After he walked the three miles back to the store, he saw the manager, Jack Engel, waiting for him at the door. "Go punch out," Mr. Engel said. When he did, Danny saw a red line scratched through his name on the schedule.

"Have your dad call me," Mr. Engel sighed as he pulled the apron over Danny's head with his big hands.

"What the hell were you thinking?" Danny's dad asked that evening when he got off the phone with Jack Engel.

"I wasn't really thinking anything. It's just that Mrs. Hudgins seemed like she needed some help . . . needed someone."

"Damn right you weren't thinking," his dad said. He opened a cupboard and took a brandy bottle down. "Do you think I can just keep finding you jobs?"

Danny was silent.

"Well, I can't. This is a small town. Everyone knows about you. I mean, who the hell would want to hire you?" He opened the freezer and scooped a few ice cubes into a tumbler. As though the cold air had cooled his temper, his voice softened. "I guess it's not all your fault. It's her too." He poured the brandy.

The cold, sharp sound of ice tinkling against the side of the glass pleased Danny.

"Are you listening?"

"What?"

"Come on, Danny," his dad said, his voice sounding exhausted. He took a long drink from his glass and coughed lightly. Then he pushed his fingers through his thinning hair. "Do you think maybe you shouldn't live here anymore? Do you think you could keep a job then?"

Danny shrugged but didn't say anything.

His dad took another drink, after which he shook his head slowly. "No. Couldn't do that. You'd starve to death in a week."

"I can try harder," Danny said, pained by his father's frustration.

"It's not like you're sixteen, for Chrissake. Men your age have careers, a home, even kids. You? You're losing bag boy jobs."

"I know," Danny said, shaking his head. "Just sometimes . . ."

"Sometimes what?" He took another drink of brandy.

"Nothing."

For a few minutes, his dad sat silently at the kitchen table and took short sips from his drink. Danny stood by the counter and listened to the ice in his dad's glass. Somehow it made him think about how thankful Mrs. Hudgins had been.

"I need some time," Danny's dad began with a sigh. "I think there's one more string I can pull. I just saw Harry Stein downtown a few days ago. He doesn't even owe me one, but he's a good guy." He shook his head, tipped his glass until the ice hit his lips and then stood up from the table. "Anyway, I have to get ready. Carol's going to kill me if I'm late again."

His dad walked out of the kitchen slowly, but stopped just before he disappeared into the dark living room. "We're talking about marriage more, now," he said. "I think I'd like to, but she wants to move south if we do. She says these winters are too long." He started to say something else, hesitated, and then walked out of the room.

Danny stood in the fading light of the kitchen.

* * *

Harry Stein, the midnight supervisor of Inbound Calls, walked Danny over to his station and showed him where to sit. "Everything go okay in training?" he asked from under his salt-and-pepper mustache. "Do you have any questions?"

Danny shook his head and then picked up his headset to show Mr. Stein that he knew what to do. The training had been thorough and clear. Throughout his shift, people would be calling in to purchase Caller Recognition units for their telephones. He was supposed to answer the calls and then read from the scripted sales pitch on his computer screen. "Word for word," the trainer had stressed. "Straying from the script is grounds for termination." After entering a shipping address and a form of payment, he would read the scripted farewell, enter the sale as completed, and move on to the next call.

"Nothing they do in training can really prepare you for midnights," Mr Stein said, almost proudly. "We don't get a lot of calls, but we keep the fires burning, so to speak. Your main goal on this shift is to keep from falling asleep."

Danny nodded and smiled.

"We do get little rushes though," Mr. Stein said, his voice becoming a little more serious. "They play that commercial sometimes in the early a.m. hours and, from time to time, this place can be a zoo. It can catch you off guard, so don't let yourself get too loopy."

"I'm a bit of a night owl," Danny assured him.

"Good," Mr Stein said. Then he laughed. "You'll probably get a chance to talk to some other night owls. We get some wackos — real nut jobs calling. They'll tell you..." He stopped himself abruptly. "Just try to end those calls as soon as possible."

Danny nodded.

Mr. Stein smiled and started to walk away. Before he'd gone far, he stopped and walked back. "Is your dad getting on pretty well with Carol Lutz?" he asked.

"Yes," Danny said. "They see each other quite a bit."

"Good," Mr. Stein said, smiling.

After Mr. Stein left, Danny looked around. The workspace on his right was empty. A guy with a goatee and an earring worked on his left.

"I'm Rick. First night?" he asked, catching Danny's eye.

Danny nodded. "How long have you been here?"

"I'm kind of a lifer — been here over nine months."

Danny nodded, but didn't say anything else.

"Starting to get cold already," Rick said. "My car would barely start . . . uh, damn it." He adjusted his headset and focused on his computer screen. "Thank you for calling Belltech Systems . . ."

Danny didn't listen to Rick's call. He was thinking about cold.

* * *

On one of the coldest nights in winter, Danny's mother bundled him up and took him walking to visit all of the neighbors. As he remembered, his father didn't like it.

"It's just crazy, Lucy. I don't understand why you have to . . ."

"People need to know. Somebody needs to tell them," his mother said. "It's something I can do."

His father shook his head. "I'm just tired. I mean, what's next? What if this cold snap lasts three nights? Are you going every night?" he asked. "And does he really need to go?" He motioned to Danny who watched everything from above the scarf wrapped around his mouth and cheeks.

"It's good for him to know what it's like to be cold," she answered.

"Do you know what people will say?" his father asked.

"I don't care," she said. She opened the front door and guided Danny into a cold that burned in his nostrils.

He remembered how their feet crunching the icy snow was the only sound in the frozen neighborhood, and steam and smoke rising slowly off rooftops were the only other things moving. Danny and his mother stopped at each neighbor's house and rang the doorbell or knocked. When people answered, his mother told them that they needed to turn on a faucet in their basements. "Just a drip," she said, "but enough to keep the water moving so your pipes don't freeze."

Some thanked her, some laughed, and some shook their heads and gave Danny sad looks. A few invited them both in for something warm, but his mother refused. "We have work to finish," she said. Between houses she told him that this was the most important thing she'd ever done.

Danny had other memories of his mother. One summer she had weeded vacationing neighbors' flowerbeds without being asked. Another time, after hearing about it as a fire hazard on the news, she walked through the neighborhood backyards and cleaned the lint from peoples' dryer exhausts. But there were darker memories—the weeks and sometimes months she would spend locked in her bedroom, blinds drawn, complaining of a pain deep inside her that the doctors couldn't find. "It's like I'm suddenly blind," she would say. "I can't get used to all this blackness." He recalled too the times she got in the car and just drove – the time the police called from North Dakota. And, he remembered that summer of his sixteenth birthday, when his father shouldered the bedroom door open and found her hanging from a belt in their walk-in closet.

* * *

Danny's phone rang.

"Thank you for calling Belltech Systems," he answered. "My name is Danny. Are you ready to hear more about Caller Recognition, the newest way to know who's calling your home?" he read.

"No, thank you. I mean, I already have it," a woman's voice said. "It came in the mail today. What I'm trying to do is hook it up to a rotary phone — one of those ones where the cord just goes straight into the wall. I can't figure out the directions, and the box said I could call this number for help."

"Let me put you on hold for a minute, ma'am," Danny said. He looked over the partition to get Rick's attention.

"What's up?" he asked, setting down a magazine.

Danny explained what the woman was asking for.

"Oh Christ, she's trying to hook it up to a phone that doesn't have a modern jack."

"What do I do?" Danny asked.

"Hang up. You're still new. If the guy from Quality Control happens to be listening and asks you about it, just tell him you hit the wrong button. You can milk that excuse for at least a few weeks."

Danny shook his head. "I want to help her."

Rick laughed slightly and then sighed. "All right." He showed Danny the screen with the directions for hooking the unit up to an older phone. "You'll probably still be talking to her at sunup."

Danny got back on the line with the woman and read the directions to her. He reread some sections many times and even had to paraphrase parts to make her understand. He talked her through as she stripped a few wires with a razor blade and twisted them into the corresponding wires on the unit. "I got it," she would say, and Danny would feel something like a low current of electricity in his spine. Mr. Stein even walked by once and gave him a thumbs up. After forty-five minutes, he was able to get her through the directions.

"It's on!" she said. "Thank you so much."

Danny's throat was dry, but he felt good at the end of the call. In some ways he thought that what he'd done was what he was meant to do, and he wondered if he could eventually get into the Complaint Department. He'd heard in training that they did some troubleshooting with the customers.

The rest of the night wasn't as fulfilling for him. From one o'clock in the morning until three thirty he only took four calls. In between sales, he read articles from a car magazine that he'd found in the break room.

At four o'clock Danny saw a young kid with a ponytail walk over to Rick's station. He could hear them talking.

"Stein shit canned me."

"Why?" Rick asked.

"This woman called up and said she wanted to get Caller Recognition because there's this old boyfriend that's practically stalking her. She wants to know when it's him calling because he's really got her scared. She said sometimes he'll call as late as two in the morning, and she has to answer because she's got this sick mother. She has to pick up because it might be her calling. Anyway, after she told me everything that was going on in her life, I just said 'That sucks'. Then I finished the sale. Stein fired me for using profanity. "

Danny tried to listen to the rest of their conversation, but his phone rang and he had to take another call. He made sure to stick strictly to the script.

Harry Stein walked over to Danny's station as the sleepy morning shift was finding its way in at seven. "You can tell your dad you did fine . . . just fine," he said.

Danny took his headset off and smiled.

"QC even listened to a few of your calls and said you sound like a natural," Mr. Stein said.

"So, welcome to hell," Rick said as he stood and stretched his back.

"All right, Rick, never mind," Mr. Stein snapped. "Unlike you, maybe Danny wants to make something of himself — maybe get on the day shift in Outbound Calls and get a few sales bonuses." He said the last part to Danny, and his voice rose at the end as though asking a question.

Danny nodded. He was too tired to ask about a position in the Complaint Department.

"All right, go home," Mr. Stein said kindly. "Tell your dad you did real good — tell him I said you did good."

Danny opened the back door and found his dad sipping coffee at the kitchen table. The room smelled pleasant — perfumed.

His father turned around. "Well, there he is. How'd it go?"

"It can be a little boring most of the time," Danny said, "but Mr. Stein said I did pretty good."

"Really? Good. That's great. Do you think . . . I mean, do you think it's something you could enjoy, maybe stay with for awhile?"

"It's okay. It was only the first night." A yawn took him for a moment.

"Do you want a cup of coffee?" his dad asked eagerly.

"No, I don't like it."

"I'm sure it's something you'll get to like. I worked midnights for *Bunny Bread* one year when I was twenty-five. Your mother used to make me two thermoses of coffee for the shift," he said. "She used to really like taking care of me."

Danny shrugged and nodded.

"Well, I hope this is something you'll stay with. I've pretty much called in all my markers. It's a good job, really — better than bagging groceries. Sometimes things happen for a reason."

"I don't know, maybe," Danny said, yawning again. When he blinked, his eyelids felt like sandpaper. Then the ceiling creaked above him with the sound of footsteps. He looked up.

"Oh," his father said sheepishly, "Carol stayed over last night." He stood up, walked over to the oven and moved a frying pan from a back burner to a front. "She'll be hungry."

Danny knew that in the three years his dad had been seeing Carol, she'd never stayed the night, although his father had stayed at her place many times. It occurred to him that she might have never stayed over because he was always there—in the way. He started to walk out of the kitchen.

"Danny?" his father called behind him. "Don't do anything . . . well, just don't . . . just try to do things the way they do things."

"I will," Danny said.

"Good morning, Dan," Carol said as she met him on the landing. She was wearing one of his dad's old bathrobes.

"Hi," he said. Her legs distracted him, flashing from under the loosely tied robe.

She reached and touched him on the forearm as she walked by. Her touch was very warm, and he could understand why his dad would want to have that touch around. Stopped on the bottom step, he watched her walk up behind his dad at the stove and wrap her arms around his thick belly.

"How'd he do?" she asked.

"Stein told him good," he said, reaching with his right arm and pulling her around to him.

Danny watched them hold each other for a few seconds and then went to bed for most of the day. He was surprised that his performance at a job was something Carol and his dad discussed. As sleep began to take him, he vowed that he would try to keep this new job, at least for their sake.

* * *

The next evening Danny tried to focus on his work, but the first few hours were very slow. By two o'clock, he started to reread the car magazine he'd read the night before. He wished someone had left a newspaper in the break room so he could have started pricing apartments.

At two thirty, Harry Stein stood up in the supervisor's station. "Here we go! This is why we're here," he shouted. Suddenly every telephone started to ring. After a slight hesitation, "Thank you for calling Belltech Systems" echoed through the room in unison, and then the harmony broke up as the nine operators fell into their own pacing. "I don't want to see anyone going on standby until we knock out this rush," Mr. Stein shouted as he put his own headset on.

Danny's first call went very well. After the scripted pitch, the customer admitted that he had only called out of curiosity, but Danny used a follow-up pitch he'd learned in training and was able to cement the deal.

"Are you sure you don't want to reconsider, sir? The trial offer price won't be around forever," he'd said.
"All right. What the hell. You talked me into it."

Danny hoped that Quality Control had been listening.

He picked up his next call. "Thank you for calling Belltech Systems. My name is Danny," he said, trying to make his voice sound more genuine. He continued to read the script but realized after a minute that he hadn't heard anything from the other end of the line. "Hello? Is someone there?" he asked.

"I'm here," a woman's whispery voice finally said.

"Ma'am, are you trying to reach Belltech Systems?"

"I just called to listen to your voice . . . some nights I need to," the woman said.

Danny wasn't sure what to do. "Do you want me to keep reading?" he asked, but then knew immediately that it wouldn't be a good idea.

"Alright," she said. "I'll listen."

He felt a hot drop of sweat roll across his ribs, but kept reading. For nearly a minute and a half he explained the benefits of Caller Recognition to her. Then the script required a question. "Would you like to hear about the easy three-part payment plan?" he asked.

The other end of the line was silent.

"Ma'am?"

"Are you allowed just to talk?" the woman asked.

"No, I wish . . ." Danny started. He listened to the din of the operators around him and felt bad that he wasn't helping with the rush of calls. He also realized that he was no longer in script and began looking for an icon on his screen that would help him end the call. "Really, I can't," he finally said.

"I'm sorry, Danny," the woman said, her voice cracking into a sob, "I shouldn't have called."

"No, wait," he said, but regretted it as soon as he'd said it. Moving his mouse, he found the "Changed Mind" prompt and began reading the words that scrolled onto his screen. "Ma'am, I'm sorry that you've changed your mind about Caller Recognition. Of course, our 1-800 number is available to you 24 hours a day should . . ."

"I'm sorry," she interrupted. "I'll hang up."

"No . . . I mean, what do you want to say?"

For a moment there was only silence. "Have you seen a single headlight in the blackness of the highway?" she started. "What if . . . I mean . . . it can go out. Then it's just darkness. I feel I might be there . . ." She stopped to take a deep breath.

"I'm not sure . . ." Danny began. She was talking like his mother used to talk, saying the same kind of thing his father used to dismiss as just "crazy talk." Danny glanced over towards the Quality Control station and thought he saw the operator squinting at him from across the room. His forehead tingled with heat.

"It's dark here, Danny. I have all the lights on, but it's dark," the woman nearly moaned.

"Why's it so dark?" HE asked, the question slipping out of him.

Before she could answer, Harry Stein stood up again at the supervisor's station and drew Danny's attention. Cupping one hand to his mouth, Mr. Stein covered the mouthpiece of his headset with the other. "We still have eighty-seven calls in queue," he shouted. "Keep 'em moving." Then, he slipped back down into his call.

Just seeing Mr. Stein reminded Danny that he was supposed to end non-sales related calls as soon as possible. "I can't talk," Danny said. He felt sick to his stomach, but thought of his father and Carol Lutz. They needed him to keep this job.

"Nobody can ever talk. We go through this life alone," the woman said.

Her words were dark and lonely like his mother's had been, especially near the end. *Is she in that much pain?* Danny thought.

"Are you there?" the woman asked.

"Yes," Danny said. Listening for a moment, he could hear the operators around him moving quickly through their scripts as they tried to get to the next sale. He knew he had to end his call. *I can't lose another job* he thought. *If she really wanted help, she wouldn't be calling me. I'm not a counselor.* He remembered her saying that she had called other nights. *Probably nothing . . . probably nothing every time she calls.* Even if she really was going to do something to herself, he convinced himself that there was nothing he could do about it. He looked over towards the QC station and was now sure that the operator was staring his way. *She just sounds like a nut,* Danny thought. *I mean, I'm not even sure she's going to do something.* The only thing he knew for sure was that he could get fired. And that would only make things harder for his father and Mrs. Lutz. Maybe they'd never get married. He thought of himself trying to explain losing another job to his dad.

"Danny?" The woman's voice sounded faded, almost ghostly. "I just want to talk to you about Jesus. Why do you think He left me in the dark?"

"I don't know," he finally said. Following the impulse of his next thought, he watched his own finger reach down and press a button. The phone went dead. Something switched inside of him too, and he needed to breathe deeply for a moment to keep from vomiting. Looking down, he could see that a call that was queued into his station was already on its fourth ring. Without thinking anymore, he pushed the button and read the company script.

Jeff Vande Zande

Emergency Stopping

Jeff Vande Zande

I.

"Sounds pretty dangerous to me," Max Hurely said as he opened the small safe behind the bar.

"I don't think I was in too much danger this morning. *A mom with two kids?*" Jack Johnson returned. He looked around the bar. It felt odd to him to be sitting at a bar again, almost risky. Distracted, he didn't think to blow on his coffee and burned his upper lip on the first taste. "Damn it! That's hot. Why do you make it so hot?"

Max didn't answer right away. Jack watched him move a handgun from the safe to its place under the cash register.

"Customers like it hot," Max finally said when he released the weight of the weapon. "And I'm not just talking about the mom with two kids. It's the whole thing. You do it around Flint, don't you?"

Jack nodded. "I've gone as far south as M-59, but mainly I'm on 75 and 69. Got up toward Saginaw a few times, too. Sometimes I just end up going for a ride. Like last week, I ended up in Grayling and watched a guy fly fishing for over an hour. On the way home though, I did help a woman with a flat." He looked out the front window through the neon twisted into the names of beers. The sky was growing lighter, and he realized he had never seen it do that while sitting on a barstool.

"*Flint*, though." Max shook his head. "You stop for any car?" he asked.

Jack watched Max step over a few feet and feel around in the darkness under the bar. "I don't stop if the car is empty," he said.

Max pulled out a remote control and used it to turn on the televisions around the bar. He flipped all of them to a channel with a morning news program, but he kept the sound low. "I mean, you're stopping for blacks, too?" he asked.

"I'm stopping for anyone."

Max turned up the volume when he saw a visual to the left side of the news anchor. The image showed the chalk outline of a body and underneath in bold words *Murder on the West Side.*

" . . . was pronounced dead at Detroit Receiving Hospital an hour after his arrival," the anchor's voice rose into the bar in proportion to the thumping of Max's thumb on the remote control. "His wallet was found on one of the teens that police apprehended. It had six dollars in it . . ."

Max worked his thumb again, and the rest of the broadcast doppled away like sound past an open car window. He shook his head while reaching into his front pocket for his cigarettes. "Heard on the news that we're raising more sociopaths than ever."

Jack ran his open fingers across his bald head, a habit he'd developed when he had hair. "Look at your windows," he said and made a sweeping gesture with his hand towards the televisions. "Watch that stuff long enough, you'll believe we're all out to kill each other." He could hear Max's wife moving around in the apartment above the bar, and he was glad because he knew she'd come down to make breakfast. Knowing she was coming helped him stop thinking about ordering a drink. Since he'd started talking to Max, his mouth had begun watering for something stronger than coffee. "Most people aren't out to hurt anyone," he said, but his eyes seemed to search for something on the floor.

Max leaned his weight against the bar. "Why'd you start doing this anyway?" he asked. He touched a flame to his cigarette and then watched it burn down the stem of the match.

Jack hadn't planned to come into Max's bar, but the diner where he usually ate breakfast had gone out of business. For the past two weeks he had tried to cook up eggs or oatmeal for himself at home, but he'd taken all of his meals on the road for the last twenty-eight years, and his small house was just too quiet. In it, he thought too much — thought too much about how alone he had let himself become. Still, he had no idea Max would ask so many questions. When Max had asked him what he'd been doing lately, he had absently told him the truth.

"You know, I know exactly why I started," Jack began, his voice unsteady. "Could never get it out of my head . . . the image, the thing I saw." The words came with difficulty for him. He was used to more of a script, a pitch. Talking about this now made it seem foolish, like a boyhood dream. He set his coffee down. "Selling that pool cleaning equipment took me all over mid-Michigan – mainly to motels and hotels though. I must have seen hundreds of cars, hell maybe thousands, broken down on the side of the highway. See people crouched under hoods, or going through trunks, or just kneeling next to jacked up tires – sometimes on both knees like they were in a pew or something. I never really thought much about them until about two years ago, after my kid sister finally had a baby."

"That's about the time you stopped coming in here," Max said.

Jack wasn't sure what had made him think of pews. He hadn't been in one since he was a kid.

"Jack?"

"Hmm? Yeah, I guess that was about the time. Like I was saying though, I was driving up to Bay City because they were opening a new hotel, which always meant a chance to make real money. I remember because the district manager really threw me a bone on that one . . . let me go even though my sales weren't so good anymore. It was July, hotter than hell. Almost as hot as this coffee."

Max smirked while Jack stopped to take a sip.

"Up on 75, just past Miller Road, the highway dips into a deep curve, and there she was," Jack continued. "This huge woman standing next to this rusted-out Caddy. She must have weighed two fifty. Her face was shiny with sweat. Probably wouldn't have thought much of her at all, but she was holding this baby in her left arm. Little thing, maybe two months old. Christ, it had to have been ninety-five degrees that day, and there she is standing in the sun with that little baby all pressed up against her. No bottle, no cell phone. She was just swaying back and forth and bouncing a little, standing back near the trunk."

He heard Max's wife come down the stairs and into the bar's kitchen.

"Paula? Could you throw together some scrambled eggs and sausage? Skillet's hot already. Jack Johnson is out here. *Just for breakfast.*" Max shouted, but he didn't look at Jack after saying the last part.

"Alright, give me a minute. I just got down," Paula shouted. Words came through her throat as though going over sandpaper.

"The hood wasn't even popped," Jack continued. "She was looking at the cars going by, but you could tell she'd given up the hope of anyone stopping for her. Her eyes seemed kinda glassy and her lips were moving, like she was whispering to the baby or maybe praying. She didn't even know enough to get out of the sun."

Jack watched Max begin counting his starting cash into the till. He tapped his cigarette on the ashtray, and the cherry snapped off, but he didn't notice. After a moment he looked up at Jack. "What? I'm listening. Go ahead."

"Forget it."

"Come on. I got a business to open up this morning. I can listen while I work. I *am* a bartender." He took a drag on the dead butt, shrugged, and then dropped it into the ashtray. He began to fish for another.

Jack could hear his breakfast frying, but he no longer felt hungry. "Anyway, she's always stuck in my mind. I mean, I didn't stop for her either – just another of the hundreds of cars that went by in a blur. Could have helped her, too. I learned a helluva lot about fixing cars after all those years on the road. In that heat, that baby could have died. Might have. I thought about that all of the time." Jack took another drink of his coffee.

"Don't remember anything in the news about a woman losing a baby to the heat," Max said. His tone challenged more than it comforted.

"That doesn't matter," Jack returned. "It's just always stayed with me that I didn't do anything. I just had to get up to that sale. Didn't even get it."

Max went to the doorway of the kitchen and looked in.

"It's coming," Paula said.

"Eventually all of my sales dropped off," Jack continued, his voice almost ghostly. "Company tried to put me at a desk taking sales calls that the younger guys called in. The hell with that. I left, but I couldn't give up the driving. Everyday I'd take long drives, and eventually I saw someone on the side of the road. I stopped, and I've been stopping for anyone for about three months now."

Max shook his head, but he looked at Jack respectfully. "You got the time. You should take up golf. That's what I'm going to do. Get out on the course and never have to see another face again. I've earned that."

Jack could hear Paula scraping his food from the skillet onto a plate. He looked at the bottles lined across the back of the bar and still wanted a drink. A few belts would make him forget about this meaningless hole he had talked himself into. Having heard himself explain it, his stopping for people seemed childish. "Max, tell her to put that in something to go," he said. He wouldn't stop at the bar again. *Not a place for breakfast* he decided.

Jack opened the bar door and quickly closed his eyes against the brightness of the rising sun. Though his pupils were sensitive to the intense light, he could still feel the darkness inside of him. He felt himself longing for what Max had—the familiar, weathered love of a good woman. He found a dumpster on the side of the bar and threw away his breakfast. If he just had a drink, he knew he could get back to something he could understand. *Then I could sit still for a few minutes without so much damn thinking.*

He pushed himself off of the dumpster where he had slumped and opened the trunk of his car. Inside he found it packed with everything he needed: jumper cables, a jug of water next to a jug of coolant, five gallons of gas, an assortment of fan, alternator, and timing belts (including an adjustable belt), tire plugs, a quick fix aerosol can for flats, a four-way lug nut wrench, a small box of u-joints, oil, bottles of liquids that could stop radiator and crankcase leaks, transmission fluid and sealer, wiper blades, a spare battery, a hydraulic jack, a creeper, flashlights, a 12 volt trouble light he had ordered special, flares, a fire extinguisher, two thermostats, radiator hoses, a can of dry gas, and maintenance and trouble shooting manuals for several different foreign and domestic cars. He saw his red tool chest packed into the middle of everything like a heart. Just the sight of it made him feel better, and he began to remember the faces he had helped over the past months— all of the people back on the road because of him. He could fix most problems right on the shoulder of the highway. For those he couldn't fix, he had telephone numbers in his glove box for the cheapest wreckers in most nearby towns. One mechanic in Flint even offered a ten percent discount to any customer who could recite Jack's license plate number, and Jack could usually help people memorize it before the tow truck arrived. This winter he planned to buy a four-wheel drive truck with a winch because he guessed that most of the cars he'd be stopping for would be stuck in snow banks or down in ditches. *A lot of people will need me* he thought. He felt warmer and then realized that the spring sun had burned off the chill of the morning.

He closed the trunk and slid into his car behind the steering wheel. Opening the glove box, he found the small journal he had begun to keep. In it he recorded the cars he had stopped for. His early entries were short and simple, usually only giving the date of the stop, the time, the make of the car, and the problem, though lately he had started leaving room for brief comments. He read over a few. "Wasn't the battery, was the starter." "Guy had a poodle that growled at me through the windshield." "Another guy stopped, too. Couldn't help with the car, but he kept the old lady calm so I could work." "Driver was a real looker and called me her guardian angel." The last made him smile. Turning his key, he listened to his engine turn over and then idle down into a smooth churn. While he waited for the temperature gauge to rise some, he counted ninety-four entries in the journal. The number made him happy, and he shifted into drive and headed toward the interstate —just in time for the morning commuters.

He took side streets toward the highway and watched people leaving their families to go to work. Garage doors rose into rafters and cars backed down driveways. When he could see people, they were often men, and on all of them he saw ties knotted up tight against their throats, the ends swinging back and forth like pendulums. Still watching the houses, he noticed the faces of children pressed against picture windows. Their little eyes strained to watch their fathers drive away. Other children were strapped into the back seats of cars on their way to daycare.

This is what I should have done Jack thought *Why the hell didn't I have a family?* Before he could sink too far into regret, he saw the sign for the on-ramp that would lead him up onto the northbound highway toward Flint. He felt suddenly better, somehow relieved.

As he made his approach, he hit the gas and got ready to merge into the blur of traffic. No other drivers shifted lanes to let him in, but he found accidental space and took it. Around him other drivers talked on cell phones while drinking coffee or fixing their hair. Others drifted in and out of lanes without the warning of turning signals — some weaving their way through at ninety miles an hour. Some were lone drivers racing down the carpool lane, but most of the drivers just stared ahead blankly, eyes fixed between the lines. When he had been racing to his own sales calls, Jack had never really noticed the other drivers. More than anything, they had just seemed in his way. Now he saw how everything about the morning commute was robotic.

Men and women climbing inside machines . . . becoming machines. *Maybe it'd be different if we all rode buses to work* he thought.

Two miles later, coming over a small rise, he saw the dim red pulse of hazard lights on the side of the highway pumping weakly into the intensity of the risen sun. The hood was up on the stranded car, and a man stood on the driver's side shaking his head. Suddenly the man's foot reared back and kicked the door. Something in the kick made Jack sad, but he laughed at the same time. Slowing, he edged his way onto the shoulder and popped his trunk. He had the man on his way again in twenty-five minutes.

II.

Jack Johnson walked out of his sister's house and felt how much the temperature had dropped. He could feel the cold burning in his nostrils. The night was bright and still under a waning moon, and the only sound he could hear was the crunch of his feet across the icy driveway. He'd only been at his sister's place for three hours, but his truck's battery struggled to turn over the engine, as though the vehicle had sat in the cold for days. While he waited for the truck to warm up, he looked at the apple tree in the front yard. A few frozen apples still clung inside the web of stark branches. An empty bird feeder dangled among them. While visiting earlier that fall, he had watched chickadees flutter around its brief gesture of charity. It reminded him of hearing a disc jockey that morning warning pet owners to bring their animals in after five o'clock.

The nights were falling as low as thirty degrees below zero. The cold snap had hit the town about a week ago, and Jack thought that in that time he must have jump started at least forty-five dead batteries for people. Lately he'd just park his truck at the mall, and within fifteen minutes he'd spot someone lifting and propping a hood among the acres of cars. He wondered how many people he'd helped, and so opened his glove box and flipped through his journal. Idling in his sister's driveway, he found himself counting back to the beginning and couldn't believe the sum of six hundred and sixty-five. Smiling to himself, he shifted into reverse.

Driving toward the highway, he looked at the Christmas lights framed around houses and strung through trees in front yards. He'd laugh at some – so many lights, as if someone were trying to turn night into day. Some front doors glowed with slogans: *Merry Christmas to All, Season of Love, Peace on Earth*. Despite the lights, the houses still looked empty—no silhouettes passing by the windows or moving in the dull gray glow of the televisions. Jack wondered what his own dark house looked like from the street. Thinking back over the evening, he pictured his sister with her husband and their child. The little boy had teased him with a candy cane, but when Jack had faked a sad face, the boy had turned sympathetic and offered the swirl of sugar in earnest. "Please take it Unca' Jack," he had begged. The thought of it made Jack suddenly lonely, and he wondered if he should have tried harder to get married and have a family. The idea of going back to his lonely house haunted him. He'd had a sip of champagne at his sister's, and its warming sting still burned in his throat. At a red light he thought about going to Max's bar for a shot and to see who was left of the old night gang.

"One drink to celebrate the season," he said, and his voice sounded unfamiliar to him in the still, cold cab of the truck. The engine had been running for over twenty minutes, but when he ran his hand across the vents of the dashboard, he could feel that the air breathing out was barely lukewarm. *It's got to be well below zero already* he thought and then mapped out in his head how a quick turn onto the interstate would get him to Max's ten minutes faster. A few seconds later, something like a gunshot exploded under his truck, and the front end lurched violently over into the other lane. Realizing he'd hit a gaping pothole, Jack steered the truck back between the lines. The pothole was one he had seen a road crew filling earlier that spring, but the freeze and thaw of winter had brought it back.

On the highway, a few intermittent headlights passed him on the other side of the median, but he was alone on his side. As if they were days from his life as a salesman, he watched the white dashes that divided the two lanes flit into the glow of his headlights and then disappear behind him in the darkness. *If only I'd a met the right woman* he thought *maybe I wouldn't be so damn lonely.* He'd had women in his life on the road, but he'd never call any of them girlfriends. Still he thought longingly of one — Carla, a woman he knew years ago in Saginaw that he had called any time he was staying in the area overnight. He had to pay her, but she always stayed afterwards and talked. He still could hear her voice, like something thick he could pull around himself and get warm. She was the only one he went to regularly — others in other towns he learned of from other salesmen, but he never went back to the same one twice. But he liked listening to Carla, and he wondered now if he had called her more for the talking than the sex. He remembered lying in bed next to her afterwards, when she would talk about her life — how her family had struggled in Georgia or about the bad men she'd met. Men with cruel mouths, knuckles, belts, lighters. He'd stare up into the darkness of the room and listen, and the darkness of her life made the darkness of his seem less so.

One night during a bad storm she had decided to stay over in his motel. When he woke at three a.m. and found her sleeping on the bed next to him, he stroked her hair and thought that maybe he loved her. Thinking of her now, he wondered should he call her again, but laughed at the idea of starting a relationship at his age. Then he nearly cried. Tonight he wouldn't be able to drive past Max's bar without stopping.

As he slowed to ease the truck towards the off-ramp that would spiral him down, he spotted something moving on the edge of the highway. His headlights swept over, and Jack was surprised to see it was a man hitchhiking. The hitchhiker held out his frozen thumb, while his other hand was jammed inside the pocket of a black windbreaker.

He was wearing a Detroit Tigers baseball hat. *Christ* Jack thought *this guy's dressed for golf.* The hitchhiker smiled kindly enough into the high beams, but his hungry stare penetrated through the light, the windshield and into Jack's eyes. Although the look made him uneasy, Jack knew he couldn't leave the man abandoned on the highway – not on a night like this. He pulled over onto the shoulder, stopped, and shifted into reverse.

He drove backwards, looking over his shoulder. For a few seconds he saw nothing. Had the man just disappeared? Then he saw a silhouette jogging out of the darkness into the dim halo of the truck's rear lights. The man's face soon loomed in the passenger window. He tried the handle, but the door didn't open.

Jack leaned over the seat and unlocked the door. When the door opened, the man slid in quickly and closed it behind him. Cold followed him in, and Jack shivered in it. The other man didn't look at Jack or say anything, but stared ahead into the darkness, blowing into his hands and rubbing his arms. Jack could see dull red splotches on the man's face where he'd probably been frostbitten.

"I can't even feel my toes," the hitchhiker said into the windshield as though he knew Jack's thoughts. Frost fell from his mustache.

"I know, it's cold," Jack said, "Anywhere I can drop you off?"

"Drop me off? I've been waiting for you all night," the hitchhiker said. He blew into his hands again and shook his head as though he were lamenting something. He stared straight ahead while rubbing his fingers together for nearly a minute.

"Look, if you know where you're going, I'll take you there," Jack said.

The hitchhiker didn't say anything. His eyes looked glazed over.

"Do you think you should go to the hospital?" Jack asked after a minute, thinking that the cold may have made the man delusional. Looking at his blank stare, he wondered if the man was mentally ill.

"Hospital? Last guy that stopped for me made it clear that I would have to pay for gas. Kind of an asshole. Not you, though," the hitchhiker said, mumbling the last part. He blew into his cupped hands again for nearly a minute and then shoved them into his armpits.

"You might have hypothermia," Jack said, uncomfortable with the long pauses. He could hear some fear in his own voice and cleared his throat.

"Christ, you are a saint. But you're a stupid sonuvabitch, too. No offense, but you don't even know what I'm going to do, do you?" He pulled his hands out of his armpits and began to clench and release his fingers. "Didn't know if I'd get them to move again," he said, smiling.

The sheepish smile bothered Jack, and he now felt something about the man wasn't right. "Alright, listen . . ." he started.

The hitchhiker's right hand slipped inside his jacket and then as quickly came out again.

Jack looked down at the gun clenched inside the other man's fist.

"Gotta wait so long for anyone to stop anymore," the hitchhiker said, shaking his head. "It's almost not fair."

"I don't keep much cash in the truck," Jack said. Something like brandy was flooding just below the surface of his skin. He felt hot and confused.

"Money? No, I don't do this for money. I don't even take the money. I just have to do it." The hitchhiker paused for a moment and looked ahead into the darkness. "If I don't, it's hell."

Trying to pray, Jack could only recall *Our father who aren't in heaven, hollow be thy name*, but that didn't sound right to him. Lost, he stared into the dim lights of the dashboard. Everywhere else was darkness.

"I'm really sorry about this," the hitchhiker said, looking down and rocking the gun slightly from side to side.

Jack looked for headlights anywhere ahead of him or in his rearview mirror, but the highway was dead.

"What the hell were you doing stopping for me anyway?" the hitchhiker asked.

"I stop for people . . . people who need help. There was this woman and a baby . . ." Jack's words trailed off. "I don't really know why I stop."

"Well, it's a good thing you did stop," the hitchhiker said, sounding grateful. "I coulda died."

On Earth As It Is

Jeff Vande Zande

Michael heard knocking, far away, as though from the distant end of long hallway. He didn't look up.

"Father?" a woman's voice asked.

Michael jumped slightly, thought to hide his glass of brandy, and then took a quick drink from it instead. "I'm here," he said. He began to stand and was surprised to see a young woman leaning through the doorway.

"You're busy," she said. "I can come back."

"No," he said and slumped back into his seat. Across the desk he had spread the church's bills, where he'd been staring at them for the past half hour. "Come in." He guessed that the woman was probably in her mid-twenties.

She stepped the rest of the way into the room. Holding her hand, a small boy toddled in behind her.

Michael stared at the blonde child for a moment. He recognized his face from somewhere. Then he looked up again at the woman. "Are you here to see me?" he asked.

"I am, but I don't have an appointment," she said. She let go of the boy, and he stepped quickly to the desk and rubbed his hand curiously along its edge.

Nobody ever makes an appointment, Michael thought.

"Tyler," the woman said as the boy's tiny fingers stretched towards a ring of keys.

"Is he around two?" Michael asked. He reached across the desk to try to grab the keys, but knocked them to the floor instead.

The woman picked them up before the boy could get them and dropped them into Michael's hand. When the keys disappeared, a whiny noise wound up out of the boy like a grating siren.

"That's enough," the woman said sharply, and the boy came to her sheepishly and was quiet. She set a diaper bag next to the guest chair. "He's twenty-six months," she said.

"Please, sit down," Michael said, watching the boy hang on her leg. He went to take another sip of his drink, but found the glass empty.

When she was seated, Michael thought to ask her if she wanted coffee, but stopped when the boy tried to lift her shirt. She pushed his hands away. When he tried again, she leaned over, reached into her bag, and pulled out a tiny cup with a lid.

"Juice, Tyler," she said. The boy pulled himself up into her lap, grabbed the cup, and then laid back into her bent arm.

Michael could see the boy smiling at him from behind the cup. "Want coffee?" he asked the woman, even though he didn't have any made.

She shook her head. "We don't really have a lot of time." She looked down at the boy.

Michael could see that the child's eyes were getting glassy. *Where to begin with the woman?* he wondered. The sound of Tyler's throat ticking as he worked at the juice filled the silence of the room.

"Father?"

"Well, I'm not sure why you're here. I don't think I've ever seen you in church before," Michael said.

The woman's face reddened.

Michael ran his hands through his uncombed hair and then stopped when his fingers reached the smooth skin of his balding spot. He examined it for a second with his fingertips, guessing it the size of a drink coaster.

"I'm Alice Fish," the woman finally said. "My mother thought I should come talk to you."

Michael guessed that her mother was Helen Fish, one of the few regulars that showed up for Sunday Mass. Glancing down, he saw Tyler's eyes close, open weakly, and then close again. He studied the boy's small features. His lips and nose seemed impossibly small and helpless. He felt a strong urge to hold him and then suddenly remembered where he'd seen him before. "Your mother comes here every Sunday and always brings him," he said.

Alice nodded.

Michael looked at the boy again, but then was distracted by the numb, tingly feeling in his cheeks. He opened and closed his mouth a few times until the feeling faded.

"My mom likes you – likes your services," Alice said.

"She does?" Michael asked.

"She said it's not so much what you say but the way you say it. She says it seems like you've been through a lot – like you know something about bad times."

Michael wondered if Alice's mother had heard something.

* * *

Two years ago in Farmington Hills, Lisa Tosh, the daughter of a Ford executive, and her fiancé had asked Michael to do the service at their wedding. Surrounded by four thousand dollars worth of flowers, Michael took the kneeling couple through their vows. In his sermon he talked about transcending the self for the needs of the other. Watching the older heads in the audience nod, he knew they were the best words he'd ever written. For the first time in years, he actually felt that something he'd said mattered.

Afterwards, at the reception, over the course of a long meal, of which he ate very little, Michael had five glasses of wine.

"Our candle's out," he said to the bride's brother and his family who were seated with him. Michael grabbed the candle and began to stand.

"I can light it, Father," the brother offered.

"No, I'll light it off their candle," Michael said, motioning towards the bride and groom at the head table. "I have something I want to tell them."

The brother nodded and smiled.

Michael steadied himself on the backs of bridesmaids' chairs until he was standing behind the newlyweds.

They both turned and looked up towards him, with beautiful faces like angels. He leaned forward. "God is happy for this marriage . . ." he began to say, but then both the bride and groom jumped away from him. He wasn't sure what had happened, but quickly realized that though his candle was out, the wax around the wick was still hot. His hand had tilted, sending a waterfall of red wax over the bride's right side and down the groom's left sleeve.

* * *

Michael winced and shook his head slightly until the memory blurred. Though the bishop denied it, Michael guessed that it was a big part of the reason he'd been transferred to Roger's City.

"Why are you here?" Michael suddenly asked.

Alice looked down at her sleeping child and studied his face. "Do you know Andy Jackman?" she finally asked, nearly whispering.

The name sounded familiar to him and he thought for a moment. "There's a Judith Jackman that comes to Sunday service."

"His mom," Alice said. "Andy is Tyler's dad . . . not my husband though. We *were* engaged for awhile."

Michael shook his head.

"It's hard to raise him by myself," Alice said. She tried to move the cup from Tyler's loose grip, but his little fingers tightened around its handles.

"We get some money from the collections," Michael started, guessing what she wanted, "and some people donate canned goods." Since the layoff at the quarry, many people that had never come to church came to see him, but only for handouts.

"No. No. It's not money," Alice said quickly. "I do all right working at the bank. It's Tyler I worry about – I mean his not having a dad around. It's sad."

Michael ran a hand through his hair. "I think you're right about fathers, but I guess I'm still not sure why . . ."

"I've tried to talk to Andy," Alice interrupted, "tried to tell him that Tyler needs him to be around . . . at least some times. But he won't listen to me, and the last few times he got really mad. I don't think I should try to talk to him anymore . . . since the quarry pink slipped him, he's just mean."

Michael stood and moved close to the window behind his desk. He sensed what Alice was going to ask him to do and felt uneasy. "I don't know . . ." he started. Looking out the window, he saw a few men going into Jake's, a bar across the street. It seemed to Michael that most of the men in Roger's City had worked at the quarry. Many had already moved out of town to find jobs. "I guess you'd like me to talk to Andy . . . I mean at least try to," he said after a few seconds. Even as he said it, he tried to think of the best way to tell her that he couldn't.

"I wouldn't ask," Alice began, "but I've been chatting with my mom about it. We were thinking about the guys around town. You know, the wrong crowd. I knew a lot of them in high school and most of them had bad dads or no dads at all. Like Andy's old man—he took off before Andy could even walk. I just don't think that boys have much of a chance without a dad around." She breathed deeply as though she'd just finished a high school speech.

What she'd said reminded Michael of his own father, a man who had always been there for him. He'd been so close with his father that he'd made few friends throughout high school and had spent most weekends working with his dad on one project or another. Michael was only nineteen when his father was electrocuted to death while helping a neighbor rewire a guest bedroom. Lost in months of drinking, he eventually went into the seminary, just like his parents had always hoped.

He looked down at Tyler. Although still asleep, the boy was brushing his tiny fingers back and forth over the fine hair of his mother's forearm. Something about the motion nearly brought tears to Michael's eyes.

"I just know at least trying to do this is important," Alice continued. "Having had Tyler, I see my life as kind of over . . . I mean my old life where I was always feeling lost. This new life is more important . . . it's mostly for him now. I see that I have to try to give him the best chance possible."

Michael watched her face as she talked, and something about her knowledge of herself, her knowledge of her calling in the world, made her beautiful. He wanted to get her and Andy together again—wanted them to be a family. "I'll do it," he said. "I'll talk to him."

Alice explained that Andy was living with his mother again. "Do you need the phone number?"

"No," Michael said, shaking his head slowly and seriously. "Something like this should be done face-to-face."

After Alice left, Michael could feel his heart thumping, blood flooding through his arteries as though they'd been dry for years. Vowing not to drink, he began to think of what he would say to Andy. He paced the room rehearsing words in his head and absently poured himself another brandy. He shrugged. *I'll need to be relaxed when I talk to Andy, anyway.* He took a drink.

At five o'clock Michael drove over to the west side of town and down a street lined with duplexes. He found Judith Jackman's place, but was disappointed to see no cars in the driveway. Still, he decided to at least try. When he knocked, dogs inside the house started barking, but nobody came to the door. In the silence that followed, Michael looked around. He saw that each duplex had its own small front yard marked off with cyclone fencing. Unlike the others, the Jackman lawn was not crowded with toys or sandboxes or swing sets. But partially under the carport, Michael could see where somebody, presumably Andy, was in the middle of rebuilding a motorcycle. As he stepped off the porch and walked closer, he saw that whoever had been working on the bike had long since abandoned the project.

He crouched down and read the name Harley-Davidson across the tank. His own father had always spoken of Harleys as though they were divine. For a moment, he remembered the two summers he and his father had worked on Vincent Blackshadow that they'd found at a junk dealer's. In the end, the bike never did run, but Michael remembered those times with his father and often referred to them when he tried to make analogies about faith to his congregation.

He studied the bike in front of him now. Under the empty headlamp socket, the front forks were propped up on a cement brick. He looked around but couldn't see the tire anywhere. Although the seat and rear tire looked in good shape, the engine itself was only partially assembled, and wires dangled down from it like roots. Numerous engine parts were scattered in a small circle under the bike, most with a scaly coat of rust already covering them. Among the nuts and bolts, he saw some parts for which he still knew the names. *Cylinder head, carburetor, gaskets, skid plate, heat shield, clutch plate, friction disk, alternator*, he thought as he recalled each name. Lying among the parts were tools he recognized too: wrenches, a few screwdrivers, spark plug sockets, locking pliers, a ratchet, and a pair of needle nose pliers. Despite the chrome plating, a light brown of rust had started to grow on the edges of the tools also. Michael looked around. No tarp anywhere. *Why would anyone leave a bike like this to rust in the rain and coming snow?*

A car pulled into the driveway. Judith Jackman was driving it.

She parked the car and stepped out. "Father Cline," she said, her voice surprised.

"Hello, Judith."

She smiled, but the rest of her face struck Michael as scared. "Do you need to talk to me?"

"Actually," he said, "I've come to see Andy."

"Oh." Her face seemed even more frightened and the smile left it. "Has he done something?"

"Alice Fish asked me to talk with him," he said, after guessing that she probably knew about Tyler.

Judith nodded slowly. "She's come around here, too. I like her, a nice girl . . ." Her voice trailed off.

"Can you tell me where I can find Andy?" Michael asked. "Will he be home soon?"

"He's on his route," she said.

"His route?"

"He drives a rural route for the Presque Isle Newspaper," she explained timidly.

"When does he get back?" She seemed frail to him, very different from the woman who loudly sang hymns off-key on Sundays.

"He doesn't usually come back . . . I mean, not right home. I mean, he's probably done with the route by now and is over to Bucky's. He'll be there until late."

Bucky's was one of the town's rundown bars. He nodded. "Thank you." He started towards his car.

"Father," Mrs. Jackman's voice eventually called to his back.

He turned around.

"He's not a bad man or a drunk. He was going to stay with that girl and help raise their boy . . . talked about it a lot. But when that quarry laid him off, and it's been six months now . . . well, he changed. I mean, getting her pregnant like that was a mistake, but he was owning up to it . . . that job, though, losing that job. It got to him. The quarry's one of the only good jobs around here."

Michael nodded. "I know." He started towards his car, stopped, and then turned toward Mrs. Jackman again. "Is that bike Andy's?" he asked, pointing with his chin toward the Harley.

"Yeah. He's had it since he was sixteen . . . dragged it out of the garage again right after the layoff."

Michael smiled sympathetically and shook his head before turning back toward his car. He imagined Andy, or more a silhouette of him, kneeling next to the bike with a wrench, and Tyler crouched next to him.

Michael parked his car across the street from Bucky's. The small brick building looked more like a bomb shelter than a bar with its few tiny windows tucked up high near the corners. Unlike the other bars in town, the cars in front of Bucky's were rusted-out models, all a decade old. A muffler hung down from under one, and another's driver's side window was filled with cardboard instead of glass. A bumper sticker on a Blazer read, "St. Patrick's Day's for amateurs. I'm drunk year-round!"

Adrenaline churned in Michael's stomach and left a metallic taste in his mouth. He was surprised by how afraid he felt. Finally, he opened his door and walked across the street. *What's going to happen to me, anyway?* he thought, running his finger along the curve of his collar, *I am a priest for God's sake.*

Although it was a sunny autumn day, the inside of Bucky's looked like dusk, except where the windows cast a few dim rectangles of light on the opposite walls. An angry guitar solo filled the room, under which Michael heard the rumble of voices. He recognized the thick smell of cigarettes. When his eyes adjusted to the lack of light, he saw half a dozen men hunched over drinks at the bar. A few others sat in dark booths near the back, and three were playing pool. He realized that every man in the place was looking at him.

"Oh, Jesus," someone said.

Someone else laughed but stopped as Michael walked toward the bar. The bartender set down a mug and turned around. He moved his hand by the wall, and the music died away to more of a hissy whisper.

Michael could feel the way the men in the bar were watching him.

"You all right, Father?" the bartender asked, moving down to meet him.

Michael leaned against the bar. "I'm fine."

"You want a drink?"

"No," Michael said. "Well, do you have brandy?" If he had another drink he knew he could easily do what he'd come to do.

"I got a bottle of Hartleys."

Michael nodded. He could still feel the other men staring at him. The bartender came back with his drink.

"Actually, I'm looking for Andy Jackman," Michael said. He saw the man at the bar sitting closest to him whisper something to the next man.

The bartender pointed toward the pool table. "He's over there . . . the one about to shoot . . . the guy leaning over the table."

Michael looked over at the pool table and saw a lean man's back bent towards him. He didn't mean to, but he threw his brandy back like a shot. Then he thought of Tyler's face, and the image of it seemed to steady him more than the drink. "Thank you," Michael said. He began to thread his way through the tables and chairs towards the pool table.

"It's Judgement Day, Andy!" one of the men sitting at the bar shouted. A few others shushed him.

Andy stood up from sinking a ball and turned towards the bar.

"Andy?" Michael asked, making eye contact with him. His face was thin and boyishly smooth.

Andy nodded and leaned against the pool table. The other two players set down their sticks and then huddled around the pitcher of beer at their table.

"I'm Father Cline," he said, extending his hand. "I'm the priest at St. Peter's . . . the church your mother attends." He picked up Andy's partially offered hand. His palm was hot, and his bloodshot eyes looked wild. "Can we sit down?" Michael asked.

"No," Andy shook his head. "I'm fine standing."

"All right," he said. "I won't take much of your time." He paused for a second, then started again. "Alice Fish asked me to come see you." Her name sent a twitch through Andy's face.

Andy shook his head and his mouth wrinkled into an angry little grin. "Christ, she's something else."

"She wanted me to talk with you about Tyler," he continued, "your son."

"I know who Tyler is," Andy said, giving Michael a hard look.

Michael nodded. "I'm sorry, of course you do. It's just that Alice thinks the boy needs a man in his life . . . a role model," he explained.

Andy looked around the bar and exhaled a derisive laugh through his nose. "And you think I'd make a good one?"

"I don't know. She just thinks the boy's father should be in his life. She just wants . . ."

"I know what she wants," Andy interrupted. "I fucking know."

"What will you do about it then?" Michael asked. He didn't like anything about Andy, especially his hostility.

Andy was quiet for a few seconds and then looked into Michael's eyes. "Who are you? I mean what the hell is this? Alice doesn't even go to church, and now you're . . . this is bullshit!"

"There's no reason to get angry. I just . . . " Michael said.

"I really can't believe this," Andy said to himself, shaking his head. "A priest for Christ's sake. That bitch is something else." With a sharp slapping motion he sent his pool cue to the floor.

"Hey, watch it, Jackman!" the bartender shouted.

"Fuck this," Andy said and turned toward the back of the bar.

Michael could see the dim outline of a door under the red light of the exit sign. He grabbed Andy's left arm. "You can't walk away from this," he said, surprising himself.

Andy turned around again very quickly and Michael felt pain shooting through his nose before falling to the floor.

"Jackman!" he heard someone yell. Then he heard a thud and creak as the back door opened on its dry hinges. A bright light flashed into the bar. Barstools screeched back, and it sounded to him as though a few men might pursue Andy, but the back door didn't open again. After a moment, he heard a vehicle start up and spit gravel as it peeled out of the bar's back lot. Then there was silence, and he lay in it, eyes closed, both hands clutched over his nose. After a moment the bartender came over to help him up.

Hitting the brakes to avoid rearending the car in front of him, Michael winced at the sudden pain in his nose. "I've patched up a lot of guys from Bucky's," old Doctor White said as he taped Michael's nose, "but this is a first." He said the pain would last for at least a week.

Driving home from the hospital, Michael thought about how badly things had gone. He knew that he'd been too confrontational. *What kind of priest gets punched out in a bar?* he thought. He thought about the layoff and the motorcycle Andy had left to rust. *I should have gone about the whole thing differently*, Michael thought. *The guy needed some sympathy first.*

Back in the rectory he opened another bottle of brandy and lay back on the couch. He was into his second glass when he heard a light knocking.

"Hello?" Alice's voice called.

Michael propped himself up on the couch. His head tingled. "I'm in here . . . just lying down," he said. He watched Alice's silhouette move out of the half-lit doorway and disappear into the darkness of the room.

"Where are you?" she asked.

"Over here." He heard her follow his voice.

"I heard what happened. I feel so bad."

"It will heal. It's just a broken nose," he said. His watery eyes adjusted and he began to see dim features in her face.

She knelt quietly for a minute. "I knew he was an S.O.B., but I didn't think he'd ever hit a priest."

"Maybe I won't be a priest for much longer." He'd thought it before, but hearing himself say it made it seem like a possibility. Something like the flu moved through his body, and he finished the rest of his drink in one swallow. His nose throbbed when he tipped his head back.

"No," Alice said softly.

He was quiet for a moment. "It's been coming for a long time . . . I mean, it wasn't just this run-in with Andy." He could feel Alice kneeling next to him in the darkness. "I just really was hoping that I could get both of you back together . . . that maybe you'd ask me to marry the both of you . . ."

"Marry us! I don't want to marry Andy Jackman," Alice said, her voice rising.

"Didn't you want to have him in Tyler's life?"

"I did, but not like that. I don't love him," Alice said.

Michael sat quietly for a moment.

"You didn't tell him that I wanted to get back with him, did you?" Alice asked.

"No . . . No, I didn't. I really didn't have a chance to say anything," he said.

"Good. I wouldn't want him to think . . . it's just not about me and him at all."

"I'm sorry," Michael started. "It's just that for a little while the idea of you two getting together . . . I mean getting married, really gave me something to believe in. When you came into my office and talked about your life being for Tyler now . . . that was so beautiful. I wanted to do something for both of you."

"I think you did do something," she said, her voice coming from above him.

"I don't know," Michael said. He felt even more lost than he had in years. Though it had never been ideal for him, his calling had given him something. Without it, he didn't know himself at all – didn't know what he would do next.

"Father?" Alice asked.

"Yes?" He'd almost forgotten she was there.

"I saw Andy."

"What?" he asked and stopped feeling around for the bottle.

"This evening I saw his truck parked across the street from my house," Alice began. "It was dark, but I could see him sitting in the cab. I could see his cigarette."

"Did you talk to him?" Michael asked.

"No. I wasn't even sure why he was there. Then, I saw that Tyler was standing in front of the window playing with his cars on the sill. I think Andy was watching him. When I walked further into the room, the truck started up and took off."

"What do you think it means?" Michael asked after a second.

"I don't know for sure, but I never see him on my side of town," she said.

"Do you still want him in Tyler's life . . . I mean after what . . . It's just that Andy's pretty broken right now, pretty messed up." Michael wasn't sure what he was saying.

"I've seen him better than this. And I just have to believe it's good for Tyler," she said.

Michael nodded. "Yes," he said, but didn't say anything else.

"I'm going to go," she said after a time. "I'll stop in again tomorrow to see how you're doing."

"Bring Tyler," Michael said, thinking of the boy's precious face.

She said she would.

After Alice left, Michael poured himself another drink and walked over to the window. *What was Andy doing there?* he thought. He wondered if his visit to Bucky's had anything to do with Andy's change of heart. Across the street all of the parking spots in front of Jake's bar were taken. Michael watched brake lights disappear on a car that had just pulled in, and then four men piled out. Opening the door to Jake's, they vanished into the dim, hazy light. Michael shook his head. *Maybe it was just because I was a priest . . . maybe that meant something to him,* Michael thought. Running his finger over his collar, he raised his glass slightly towards where the men had just been. Then he took a long, slow drink.

Layoff

Jeff Vande Zande

The rumor around town was that this layoff was going to last a long time. Old men talked about it in the supermarket, the sporting goods store, the liquor stores. Although it was spring, men talked about the iron ore mines and the layoff as though it were winter. Paul Wolfe waited behind them in lines at fast food restaurants, and their words suggested a blizzard coming down out of Canada, crossing Lake Superior, and shutting down the whole town. He remembered one layoff from his childhood, his father talking about how friends and relatives were moving below the bridge to find work in Grand Rapids or Saginaw. Some had gone as far as Detroit, others out-of-state altogether. That layoff had lasted three years. This one they said was going to be longer.

Paul was still surprised when his supervisor called him into the office and told him he had to send him home.

"How long before I get called back?" he asked.

"Wouldn't hurt to look for other work while you're riding out the wait."

"You think I'll be back within the year?"

"Hard to say," he said, standing and walking Paul toward the door. "They're going to call back the guys with seniority first." The supervisor's voice was heavy and tired.

* * *

Walking towards his car across acres of parking lot, Paul could hear the robins that had recently returned. Their sounds usually cheered him, would send him into reveries of fishing trips and long camping weekends. Now he hated the birds. On the drive home he thought of all the things he had bought on credit: a house, a car, furniture, a bedroom set, a stereo. Slowly paying them off over months, he had always thought of these things as his. Now he realized they weren't. He thought of his wife and his kids. Though he tried to fight them, the tears slid down his cheeks.

* * *

For the first six months he collected unemployment and looked for work. During the second month of the layoff, he drove down the lakeshore to check on the status of his application at one of the power plants where he'd heard there was an opening. When he arrived, the head of human resources told him that they'd lost his application, but he could fill out another one. Angry, Paul drove home. Waking the next morning with no new prospects, he drove back to the power plant and filled out another application. His wife began to encourage him to apply for jobs out-of - state.

* * *

Most mornings Paul would drink coffee while Sandy would get Katy ready for kindergarten. He closed the morning paper. "Same damn jobs as yesterday," he reported.

Sandy waited in front of the microwave, didn't say anything. When it beeped, she removed a bowl of hot cereal and walked it over to Michael's highchair. Paul watched his wife.

* * *

Just last night they lay in bed together, and he remembered how cold the space had felt between them. And he thought that he couldn't hold her to comfort her (and himself) because she had never really wanted this. She had always wanted to move out of the Upper Peninsula to a big city where things were happening. And though he really didn't want to, they had planned on moving to Minneapolis. Then Katy was born. When Katy was about one year old, Paul's dad got him a job at the mines, which meant good money and stability. He never knew how Sandy felt about the job — he just took it because that's what he assumed a father should do. They had never really talked about their hardships but instead tiptoed through weeks of polite silences that, like aspirin, masked their pain more than healed it.

"I'm cold," she had said, but he'd only rolled over, thinking that somehow her words were simply a reproach to his new habit of turning the thermostat down at night.

* * *

For the most part the kitchen was quiet—the clink of Katy's spoon in her bowl, Michael's little rebellious whines. Through the vents Paul heard the furnace. The blower wheel dragged, screeched and then finally picked up momentum; he could tell that the motor was dying.

"It's snowing," Katy squealed. She jumped up from her seat and pushed the curtain back.

Paul looked out the window and could see the lazy flakes floating down. It reminded him of Christmas, and he opened the paper again to see if he had overlooked anything.

"They go away when they touch the grass," Katy said, her voice disappointed.

"You'll have plenty of snow soon enough," Sandy said. "Now eat up, the bus will be here soon."

Katy sat down again and ate a few bites while her mother watched. Sandy smiled at her. Michael began to cry, and she wiped his face with a small washcloth. Suddenly, Paul stood and wrestled the entire newspaper down into a tight ball and then shoved it into the wastebasket. Everyone including the baby looked at him. Conscious of himself, Paul opened the refrigerator and bent down to look inside.

"My cousin had ten years in, and he hasn't been called back yet," Sandy announced.

When Paul closed the refrigerator the bottles in the door shelves rattled around.

"We have to do something soon," she said. Her back was to him; Michael was finally eating.

"Some of these jobs I can get don't pay what I made at the mines," he said after a few seconds.

She nodded and kept feeding Michael.

* * *

Paul walked Katy out to the bus stop. She tried to catch a snowflake, told him that she wanted to take one to school.

That night another couple stopped by and haggled a hundred dollars off the price of their sofa and recliner.

* * *

By the next Monday the ground had frozen and snow covered the lawn. Paul walked Katy to the bus stop. The children called to her and she ran ahead.

Ignoring Paul, the children talked about sledding and snowmen and the upcoming holidays. Paul noticed one girl standing separate from the rest, closer to the blacktop. Tall, she looked older, maybe in third or fourth grade. He watched her staring down the road. The way she stood suggested that she knew something that the other children didn't or had decided that what they did know was childish. After a few minutes she tensed and then turned quickly to look down the street. Seeing other kids straggling out of their driveways making their way leisurely, she yelled, "The bus!" When they began to run she seemed satisfied and turned to watch the road again.

Paul leaned forward and could see the dim headlights coming toward them. Though he didn't want this world to end he could see that it was already dissolving. The children began to shrug their book bags into place and pick up their lunch buckets. They didn't speak, but drifted one behind the other into a little line, the tallest girl in front.

"Bye Katy, I love you. Have a good day at school," Paul said, his voice rising into sweetness.

"I love you too, Daddy."

The bus moaned to a stop in front of them, and the door sighed open. The children began to march up the stairs and file back to find their seats. The driver nodded to Paul and then scanned the children in his overhead mirror. When he was satisfied, he worked the clutch and gas, and the bus grunted its way up through the gears and then dropped out of sight over a hill.

Paul walked home cutting a path over the snowy sidewalk. He hoped to have some kind of work before the holidays. He had heard that some out-of-work miners, especially those that had been through the last layoff, were driving over to Iron Mountain, a small town about two hours away. The press operators had been on strike at the Iron Mountain Gazette for the past year, and the newspaper owners were offering anyone who'd cross the line twelve dollars an hour. Paul thought about going, but he heard the way the men in town talked about the scabs. They called them thieves, and now and again Paul overheard groups of men talking about individual scabs, saying, "I know where he lives." Unknown assailants jumped one man in his driveway late at night, but he swore to reporters from his hospital bed in Marquette that he'd only been visiting relatives in Iron Mountain. Windows had been smashed out of other houses, and one car was drenched in gasoline and set on fire. Paul was frightened by the situation but in some ways felt he'd never have to get into it. Unlike many miners, he had other skills to fall back on - he was certified in both HV/AC repair and welding. He felt pretty sure that he would find work. *Still, I'd cross a line if I had to* he thought.

* * *

The next Monday another two inches had accumulated on the ground. The back screen door rattled, and Paul looked out the window as a squall whipped snow across their yard. A small voice droned through the radio speaker listing the few cancellations for the morning — church events mostly.

"This ain't bad enough to cancel school," Paul announced. He circled a job in the newspaper. A local chain hotel was hiring a maintenance worker — starting pay was six dollars an hour. He also glanced through the real estate section to see what apartments were available. Seeing the same advertisements he closed the paper and watched Sandy feed Michael. He felt the heaviness that had settled between them. They didn't talk beyond common courtesies — hadn't made love in weeks.

Later while he was helping Katy into her winter coat, Paul heard the telephone ring. Michael jumped from a small nap he had fallen into in his highchair. Sandy answered the phone and then nodded to Paul, her face tinged with a slight smile.

"It's for *Paul Wolfe,*" she whispered.

He took the phone, could feel his heart thumping through his ribs.

"Hello?"

"Hello, Paul? This is Martin Rose of Gren&Dell Incorporated in Milwaukee. You sent us an application a couple months back, and we have some openings now. You're a welder, right?"

"Yeah, I'm certified." He heard his own voice rising, becoming almost childlike. Sandy stared at him from across the room, her hand closed over Katy's.

"Good, can you come down this Friday for an interview?"

"I think so." Paul's voice was hesitant. Milwaukee was a five-hour drive.

"We're starting guys at fourteen bucks an hour, and we pay overtime."

"I can be there."

The man told him where to make reservations and to call him as soon as he arrived on Friday. When Paul hung up the phone he danced Sandy around the room.

* * *

Katy missed her bus, so they bundled up Michael and drove to the school together. Paul was excited, and the rear end of the car fishtailed around corners.

"Careful Paul, not too fast," Sandy said.

"Oh, we're fine. Just gotta turn the wheel into the slides." He pumped the brakes and came to a stop at one of the three traffic lights in town.

"I think it would be fun to live in a big city – so much to do," Sandy said.

"Milwaukee's good size."

"We could go to some concerts . . ." Her voice trailed off and she unbuckled her seatbelt. Quietly, she turned around and checked on Michael in his car seat.

"I don't have it yet," Paul said, his eyes fixed on the snowy road.

"How far is Negaunee from Milwaukee?" Sandy asked as she buckled herself back in.

"About five hours."

Paul noticed that she was quiet the rest of the way to the school and then home.

* * *

That night they found each other lying in the darkness and celebrated with skin and mouths. Afterwards they cooled quietly in silence. He wanted to ask her how she really felt about possibly moving, but he thought he might disturb their perfect evening. *Better not to bring it up* he thought.

* * *

Sandwiched between two letters from collection agencies, a Gren&Dell brochure arrived with Thursday's mail. Standing by the mailbox, Paul examined the cover. About fifty employees were posed outside of the company headquarters in Madison. They struck Paul as clean people – standing straight, smiling, each with the index finger of their right hands held out in front of them to let everyone know that Gren&Dell was number one. In the background the mirrored window of the building reflected their backs, suggesting that they were only whole people because the company was behind them. He read the caption below: "Gren &Dell Inc. — helping you dig in to your future." Later, when Paul was reading through the brochure at the kitchen table, he saw a picture of the welding line where the earth-moving machines filed by. On the same page someone (probably a secretary at Gren&Dell) had pasted a sticky note with an arrow pointing to one of the welders on the line. Above the arrow was written "you!"

* * *

He left early on Friday morning. Coming into Wisconsin he watched the trees fade away into acres of farmland. The tops of cut corn stalks peeked up through the snow like stubble. To either side of him and ahead he could look out for miles. Then, nearing Green Bay he saw the fields rise into overpasses and factories.

* * *

As the interstate wound around the city, Paul noticed exits that looked familiar to him, and he remembered family vacations from his boyhood. Every January his father had always taken the family to Green Bay for a little getaway – a chance to swim in a pool and eat in restaurants. Though his mother had wanted to save enough to go to Florida at least once, his father insisted on the yearly trip into Wisconsin, which always drained their meager vacation account.

Paul could picture his mother sitting by the pool with her sad eyes. And his father came to mind, too. Always going into the sauna, or into the whirlpool, or diving into the deep end — despite the posted signs. This, after the three and a half-hour drive of his father pointing out the same tourist traps and his mother sighing. He remembered that his parents never really had spoken on car trips (or any other time), but instead just looked out their separate windows. When Paul turned sixteen his parents did begin to talk more than they ever had—sometimes yelling.

His mother now lived in Duluth with her second husband. His father, still living in Negaunee, would be leaving for his winter trip to Green Bay in about a month.

Paul wondered if he and Sandy talked enough. He decided he would call her as soon as he got to the motel and ask her if she really even wanted to move to Milwaukee. *If she doesn't, we won't* he thought, but somewhere in the seventy miles between Green Bay and Milwaukee the impulse to call her faded away.

* * *

As Paul drove into Milwaukee the snow vanished, and everything became brick, steel, and asphalt. Hundreds of road signs overwhelmed him and he had a difficult time following the directions to the motel. He nearly missed one exit when a man dragging a sled full of mufflers down the interstate's shoulder distracted him. As he pulled into the motel's parking lot, he was still thinking about him. He wondered if he were homeless.

* * *

Paul set his suitcase down in his motel room and picked up the phone. He dialed a number from a slip of paper in his wallet.

"Yeah?" said a tired voice on the other end. It was not the same person he had spoken to earlier in the week. This voice was not as friendly.

"Yes, hi. This is Paul Wolfe. I got an interview today."

"Hold on." Paul could hear the man shuffling through some papers.

"I don't have you down here."

"I'm not down?" Paul had trouble taking a breath, could feel his lungs constricting.

"No. What were you coming in for?"

"Welding." His voice was high, and he tried to clear his throat.

"Are you in Milwaukee?"

"Yes."

For a few seconds Paul heard nothing.

"All right, get here by one thirty."

"Where?" Again his voice was timid.

"Jesus, didn't they tell you anything? Take I-43 out of Milwaukee and follow it to Highway 83. Stay on 83 for ten or fifteen miles, and you'll see us on the left. You can't miss it. Just look for the Gren&Dell cars."

Paul scrambled for pen and paper and wrote down the directions. "Got it."

"All right." The man hung up.

Though at first he started to worry, he soon shrugged off the incident for what it was—a paperwork mistake. Someone had misplaced him. He had seen it happen many times at the mines—lost vacation requests, delayed pay raises, deceased spouses left on insurance policies. These were common occurrences. He looked in the mirror, cinched up his tie, and walked out to his car.

* * *

Although traffic on the interstate wasn't heavy he still felt crowded by the many eighteen wheelers passing him.

Cars eventually began to honk at him, and he noticed that he was only going fifty miles an hour. As he sped up to seventy, he missed his exit. He had to drive three miles before he could find another exit and get back on the interstate in the other direction. Glancing down he saw that it was already after one o'clock.

* * *

Without a layer of snow over them, the fields on Highway 83 struck Paul as sad and barren. The overcast sky ran all the way down to the horizon. On the edges of black fields crouched tilted barns and houses with abandoned cars rusting around them.

Ahead, Paul spotted a small cloud of dust on the right shoulder of the highway, which slowly became a teenager on a dirt bike. He began to wonder if he was on the right road; he couldn't imagine that a Gren&Dell plant was out in the middle of farm country. He decided he would signal for the rider to stop, ask him if he was on the right highway but, barely slowing, the kid dropped his right leg, leaned into a sharp turn, and raised a ribbon of dust as he sped down a gravel driveway.

Where the hell am I? Paul thought. He drove for a few more miles, haunted by the feeling that he should turn around, go back to the motel, start over. But he had nowhere to go from here, no other directions. He had this one road which he wasn't even sure anymore was Highway 83. Slowing, he looked for road signs, but the shoulders were bare, nothing to see except miles of telephone wires.

Just before he was about to turn around and backtrack to see if he had missed any obvious driveways, he finally saw a white building coming up on the left side of the road. Four white station wagons with Gren&Dell painted on the front doors were parked around it. He pulled into the driveway and parked near the back of the lot next to a black truck with Indiana plates. His heartbeat finally slowed.

* * *

Opening the door to the warehouse Paul immediately made eye contact with a bearded man across the room who indicated with a snap of his head that he should sit down in the chair next to the door. The bearded man was standing next to another man, both in white shirts, and they were watching a small forklift stacking boxes. The driver was smooth and handled his loads with precision. After five minutes, he saw the bearded man signaling for the forklift driver to cut the engine and get out. The driver, dressed in jeans and a camouflage jacket, followed the other two men to a picnic table about ten feet from Paul. The bearded man set down what looked like an application onto a neatly stacked pile. His mouth moved, and the man in the camouflage jacket nodded.

The man in the camouflage jacket started towards the door. Paul smiled at him and spotted the dull gray remainder of a black eye above his left cheek.

The man with the beard walked over soon after. "You the one thirty?"

"Yeah, I'm Paul Wolfe," he said, standing. They shook hands.

"What do you do?"

"Welder," Paul said. He looked at the pile of applications in the neat stack. "Are there still positions left?"

"If there's nothing left in welding we can get you in somewhere else." He walked towards the picnic table and Paul followed. He could feel heat spreading throughout his forehead.

"This is going to go kind of fast, we got a lot of guys to hire by Monday."

Paul nodded and felt a little relieved that the interview would be brief.

A balding man sat at the picnic table, a laptop computer open in front of him. He looked up at Paul and then pointed to a box full of applications. "Find yours. They're pretty close to alphabetical."

"His name's Paul Wolfe," the man with the beard said, then turned and walked across the warehouse floor and disappeared behind a wall.

Paul went down to the W's but couldn't find his application. Anxious, he began to sort through the papers one by one starting from the top. He felt a drop of sweat roll down the side of his ribs.

"What's your social security number?" the balding man asked.

Paul recited it as he searched a second time through the applications and could hear the man keying the numbers in.

Another man walked over, a man Paul hadn't seen before. "How many after him?" he asked, motioning to Paul as he pulled a bench out so he could sit. Paul recognized the man's voice from the phone call in the motel.

The balding man stopped and looked at the clipboard. "About fourteen," he reported.

The new man exhaled loudly.

"Found it," Paul said, relieved. He could see the bearded man walking back towards him.

"Found it? Good." He took the application from Paul's hand and gave it to the balding man who nodded slightly. "Follow me," he said.

Paul followed him to the other side of the warehouse. Behind the wall he saw a small welding station. Pieces of steel were scattered across the floor, but he noticed that a few pieces had been set in vises near a welding table.

"Put that gear on," the bearded man said, his hand pointing to a box under the table.

Paul slipped a heavy leather apron over his head, tightened a mask on his brow, and pulled the thick gloves over his hands. They were damp inside.

The bearded man saw that he was ready. "All right, I made four different seams—ones you'd typically find on the line. Weld them together."

Paul looked over the seams. None looked too difficult, just a few tight corners. Snapping his neck, he flipped the mask down over his face, and everything darkened to a small rectangle. For a few seconds he could only see the silhouette of the steel, but then he pulled the trigger, and his eyes began to follow the bright spot of the arc as it slid down the seams. Between welds he checked his work, trying to be fast but accurate. For the last weld he kneeled to get

at a tricky corner. Flipping his mask up he saw that the
bearded man was already checking the other welds.

"I can clean them up a bit," Paul said. He looked around
for a steel brush.

"No, they look fine."

He took off the gloves, and the man extended his hand
down to him. Paul could feel tension and torque in his
palm and fingers and knew that the man wanted more
than to congratulate him; he was trying to pull him to his
feet. He let his body relax, began to rise, and then slipped
out of the sweaty grip. His head cracked against the bottom
of a vise. Ignoring the hot pain, he scrambled to his feet.

"You all right?"

Paul nodded. His head throbbed.

Walking back toward the picnic table, he saw that the
other men were chuckling, and he wondered if they had
seen. Another man in jeans and a blaze orange hunting
shirt was hunched over the box of applications. He wasn't
chuckling.

The bearded man set Paul's application on the neatly
stacked pile. "We'll need you to start Monday at six," he
said. He shook his hand one last time and then walked
over near the new man. "Finding your application all
right?"

Paul couldn't hear the other man's answer — only the
murmur of words.

"We'll do your W-4 information Monday, " the balding
man at the laptop said without looking up.

"Do I come here?" Paul asked.

"No." The man looked up. His face wrinkled as he
thought for a moment. "Do you still have your brochure?"

He nodded. He could picture it on the bedside table
back in the motel.

"Okay, map on the back will take you to our downtown
plant."

"All right, I'll see you Monday then," Paul said. He
began to walk toward the door.

"Hey?"

Paul turned and saw the balding man looking at him seriously. "When you get there, just drive through the gates. We'll be looking for your car. Red Cavalier, right?"

Paul nodded, guessing that they had tight security.

"Good, see you Monday then." The man turned back to his screen.

* * *

When he arrived back at his motel he called Sandy and told her the good news. Then he explained his plan. He would stay in the motel for the week and start the new job. During the evenings he would look for a decent apartment, something they could live in until their old house sold and they could look for another. During the week she should have her brothers help her pack up the house so he could drive back the following weekend and move the whole family down.

She started to cry.

"What's wrong, honey?" he asked. He hadn't heard her cry in years.

"It's just so much . . . so fast," she said in between shaking breaths. "I mean . . . it's almost the holidays . . . my family's up here . . . your dad."

"Now I shouldn't take the job? Why the hell did I drive all the way down here?" He could hear the frustration in his own voice and tried to keep it from rising into anger.

"No, you have to take it . . . I know that. It's just a lot to think about. I'll be okay – I just need to adjust." Her voice shook less.

He told her that he could stay in Milwaukee during the week and come home on the weekends, at least until after the holidays.

"No, I'll be okay. I just need to think about everything for awhile," she said.

He told her he'd call again on Sunday. As he hung up he felt he should have kept talking with her. *She'll figure this out for herself* he finally decided.

* * *

He spent Saturday looking for an apartment. Confident, he circled eight prospects in the newspaper. Although he reached six of the landlords by phone he was only able to get to three of his scheduled showings. Driving through the city confused him: the one-way streets, the chaos of signs, the streets without signs. Of the apartments he did get to, two were too small. After seeing the third, which turned out to be an efficiency, he drove back to the motel. He decided that he had all week to look for apartments.

* * *

On Sunday he called home and spoke with Sandy. She told him she felt better about moving and said her brothers were coming on Tuesday to help her begin packing up the house.

"I won't mind moving out of this town," she told him. "I bet there are a lot of colleges and universities around Milwaukee. I could take a few courses."

"I didn't know you still thought about going back to school."

"I enjoyed the few classes I took before Katy was born," she said.

Paul was happy for her, although he thought her voice still sounded quiet and sad. After about a half hour he told her that he would call again on Wednesday. She wished him luck with the job.

* * *

Driving into the buildings of the downtown the next morning reminded him of the time he had fished the gorge, where the Ontonagon River is flanked on either side by two- hundred foot cliffs. The river he was in now, however, bubbled with flashing brake lights, and the windows of early morning offices shined in the cliff faces. *Jesus, does everyone in Wisconsin come into Milwaukee for work?* he wondered. According to the back of the brochure, the Gren&Dell plant was on fifth, and Paul had only jerked his way to tenth by 5:40. By the time he finally crossed Sixth Street, he looked at his dashboard and saw the green 6:05 glowing back at him. Five minutes late on his first day.

He slammed his fist into the dashboard, regretting it before it even landed. His index finger split open at the knuckle. Looking up from the small bead of blood, he saw the Gren&Dell plant and he could tell something near the entrance wasn't right. His mind focused the details slowly. *Ah Christ,* he thought. A crowd of people was standing in front of the gate, and police cars were parked near the high fence that ran along the sidewalk. *This can't be a strike.* The driver in front of him slammed on his brakes, and Paul just barely kept from rear-ending him. Two cars up, another driver had his signal on to turn into the crowd of people, and Paul saw that it was the black truck from his interview on Friday.

In front of the gate to the plant about fifty angry strikers shook signs and shouted. In the parking lot beyond the strikers, Paul could see white Gren&Dell cars and, beyond that, men in white shirts were moving about in a small eddy near the canopy of the plant. *Those bastards didn't even tell me* Paul thought. He then thought of his family and knew he had to cross the line. There was nothing for him back in Negaunee except minimum wage or waiting out the months—maybe years—of the layoff. If he didn't drive through the gates and take this job, it might be a long time before he and his family could live in a house again. They had grown used to the things that come with a good job—a nice television, newer clothes, two cars, vacations. A good job had helped shape he and Sandy into the people they were, and he wasn't sure that the people they would become without a good job would still want to be together. That's what scared him the most, he wasn't sure who he was anymore. For months he'd felt uprooted, torn from his name; everything he believed himself to be left him when he punched out from the mines that last time back in the spring. The sudden anonymity had fueled his rush to find another good job as soon as possible. More than anything he was afraid of the changes not having a good job would bring. *If I don't take this I could lose everything,* he thought.

The black truck rolled slowly towards the open gates, and the strikers yelled into the windshield. Paul watched their individual faces break out of the surface of the mob like whitecaps on Lake Superior. He had seen these faces before, though none of these men had ever probably been to Neguanee. These were the faces he'd always seen at company softball games, on the edges of parades, or scattered down beaches surrounded by their children. Most of them were good men, and Paul realized that they were angry because they, like him, were becoming less who they were with each scab that slipped by.

A fire barrel on the sidewalk was still throwing up flames, and Paul pictured the men who had stood around it through the cold overnight shift of the strike. Their wives, he imagined, had driven thermoses of coffee and soup to them. Their children, like his own, were in school, unsuspecting, waiting for Christmas. *These guys are the same as me*, he realized.

The bearded man from his interview ran out a few yards from under the canopy and spoke into a walkie-talkie. Suddenly, the police near the gate formed a line like a breakwall and began to push the strikers back, and their desperate, yelling faces disappeared behind the uniforms. Punching the gas, the driver of the black truck drove the rest of the way through the gates, but not before a brick arced up out of the mob.

As the brick shattered the rear window out of the black truck, Paul thought of his wife. *She cried* he suddenly remembered. When he had told her that Gren&Dell had hired him, she had cried. That she had later stopped crying, and had even said that she wanted to move, didn't matter to him. Her first reaction had not been relief or excitement, but sadness. Her crying was probably the most honest gesture either of them had made in months, maybe years.

The cars in front of him began to lurch forward, past the plant, and Paul knew he had to decide whether or not to drive through the gates. As he looked at the men he began to feel guilt—a heavy burn in his spine. Everything these men understood themselves to be was at risk, and Paul felt sorry for them and their families. He also felt the danger in the air; somebody was going to get hurt today. *Courses?* he thought. *If Sandy had wanted to take courses, she could have done that at the college back home.* He didn't know what his wife was thinking, and he decided he couldn't drive through the gates until he did.

* * *

As Paul drove past the plant he kept his eyes straight ahead, and the strikers ignored him. Two blocks down the road he pulled into a gas station and felt his entire body was shaking. Inside, he handed the cashier the last of his bills. The teenager sighed, but cracked open a few rolls of quarters and counted out twelve dollars worth. Paul closed his fist around the money and then walked across the parking lot where he huddled into the small shelter of a telephone booth. Setting the coins in stacks across the top of the phone he thought about how he would start the conversation. Down the street he could see another car rolling slowly up to the gates. Two police officers were trying to pull a striker off of the hood. Paul dropped the first few quarters in and dialed before he really knew what he was going to say. After the first ring he decided he was simply going to talk with his wife honestly. He wanted to tell her how afraid he felt—of everything. He wanted to tell her that he didn't know what he was doing and that he needed her help. He felt the warmth from his tears. Looking down the street he saw a striker holding his right arm and a police officer waving a nightstick in his face.

From the Slightest Wings

The police cars in the parking lot were not parked in spaces, but were left where the officers had jumped out. Gretchen noticed that the few cars going by on the street were moving slowly past the motel. A few minutes ago, she had watched the spinning lights of the ambulance pull out and disappear in the direction of the hospital. Looking out beyond the canopy, she watched the silhouettes of men moving around the furthest police car. A rear door opened, and she guessed it was an officer pushing the head and shoulders of the biggest of them into the back of the car. She looked at the silhouettes of the other big men, but could only make out the arms — crossing and uncrossing, going into pockets and out, scratching at shoulders. These other men, boys really, hadn't done anything, but hadn't done anything to stop him either. An officer stepped out of the darkness into the bright lights beneath the canopy. He was older, but probably still fifteen years younger than her she guessed. His eyes adjusted slowly to the light, and he squinted to find her through the glass and across the lobby standing behind the front desk where she had watched everything. He opened the door and stepped in, and she knew he was there to ask her questions. And she felt ready . . . for anything.

* * *

Gretchen Saunders had only taken the job at the motel because her husband had died six months ago and the nights early in the week were just too long to be alone. On weekends, she drove to her son's house about an hour away in Petoskey and spent time with his family, although some-times she didn't think it was fair for her to impose herself all of the time. Since Joe had passed away, she had devel-oped a need to be around people, especially at night. Most days, in the light, she could handle.

When the front desk manager called on a Wednesday and said he needed her to work Saturday night, she told him she could. In some ways she thought it would be a nice reprieve for her son's family, especially his wife. Other times, as she thought about it throughout the week, she became nervous because she had only been doing the job for a month. The manager had assured her that Saturday nights were no different from any other nights, just a little busier. Although he had told her that he knew she could handle it, his voice had sounded like the telemarketers who called all day and goaded her into buying things she didn't need.

While putting a few new seedlings into her garden on Saturday morning, Gretchen thought of Joe and her fingers stopped where they were in the dirt. Memories of him always seeped into her mind the same way. For a moment, a warm happiness at the thought of his face would take her, but what always followed was the realization that he was gone and she would be alone the rest of her life. The sadness came then, a suffering animal inside of her, palpable.

They were planning their first trip to Hawaii when his cancer was diagnosed. Two months later he was dead, four months after his retirement. He had been such a part of her and had made things easy by making most of her decisions for her. She had loved him for the way he could guide her and missed him now the way a stroke victim might lament the loss of one side of the body. Leaving her tools in the soil, she walked into the house to try to nap through the grief. She turned on the air conditioner, knowing that its hum might lull her away.

Arriving at the motel late in the afternoon, she ran her card through the time clock and said hello to Amy, the day shift clerk. The last hour of Amy's shift was the first hour of Gretchen's, but the younger woman continued to work as if she were alone. Gretchen tried to stay out of her way. Looking through the reservations, she saw that most of the guests for the evening were already checked in, and she was relieved to think that the night might not be too overwhelming. She watched Amy checking in a couple, and was surprised by how quickly the young woman swiped credit cards through the machine, punched in totals, and handed out keys.

A young man with shoulder-length hair glanced up at Amy now and again from one of the lobby chairs. Gretchen watched him as he flipped through local tourism brochures, obviously not reading them. His eyes would then wander slowly across the paintings of Lake Michigan shorelines and lighthouses until they finally came back to Amy. Sometimes she met his look and smiled at him, and Gretchen recognized the smile as one she had reserved for Joe when he used to look at her from across a room. She looked away from the young man, hating herself for how quickly thoughts of her dead husband came.

During the first hour of the shift, Gretchen had tried to keep herself busy, but had only managed to hand out a few soaps and towels. At ten minutes to five, another couple pushed their way into the lobby.

"You could at least hold the door," the woman said.

The man with her said nothing and walked to the front desk. "Room for Abbot," he said in a flat voice.

"I hope it won't be this sweltering all summer," the woman said.

Mr. Abbot said nothing. He began to shuffle through his wallet.

His wife stepped up close to the desk and looked at the clock on the wall behind it. "Is that clock right?" she asked.

Gretchen looked at the clock, looked at her own watch, and then looked at Mrs. Abbot. "Yes, it's right."

"Well, I guess we won't see any of the quilt show today," she said accusingly to Mr. Abbot. "You just couldn't take the road my dad told you to, could you?"

Gretchen knew the quilt show that Mrs. Abbot was talking about—a two-day affair at the local armory that often brought people in from around the state. She had gone a few times with friends, but never with Joe.

"The highway your dad wanted me to take ain't any faster," Mr. Abbot sighed from under his mustache, his voice too timid for his argument. He was not a very big man, probably five or six inches under six feet.

"Oh, you know everything," Mrs. Abbot said, louder than she needed to for him to hear.

"Have a good stay, Mr. Abbot," Amy said and handed him his room key.

When he took it, Gretchen noticed black scabs on his knuckles. She had seen Joe's hands looking the same way after he had been in a fight at a bar in Upper Michigan during deer season. At that time, Joe was twenty-two. Mr. Abbot looked to be in his late thirties.

He picked up his luggage and began to walk down the first floor hallway.

Mrs. Abbot followed him. "Is this the floor we're on?" she asked.

He didn't answer but stopped in front of room 107 and tried to open the door. Gretchen watched him turn the key a few times, but the door wouldn't open. Then, Mrs. Abbot grabbed his hand, twisted the key out of it, and jammed it back into the lock. After a hard turn, it opened, and Mr. Abbot followed his wife into the room. Gretchen saw his mouth say something.

"You have about three more rooms to check in," Amy said behind Gretchen. "Then, it should be pretty easy for the rest of the night."

Gretchen turned and saw Amy standing by the time clock looking hurriedly for her card.

"Are you going to be all right?" Amy asked. "Do you have any questions?" She dropped her card into the clock. It gave a metal thud.

Gretchen wondered if the front desk manager had said something to her. "I'll be fine," she said, but she felt old and silly. She turned and picked up the folder of pending reservations.

"All right. Good night, then," Amy said and walked out into the lobby. The young man who'd been waiting for her stood as soon as he saw her on the other side of the desk. While he slipped an arm around her waist she untied the scarf from her neck. They walked towards the doors.

Gretchen watched them, wondering if she should have taken the time to think of a few questions for Amy. *I don't even know what to tell people who come in after all of the rooms have filled* she thought. The most rooms that had ever been filled on a Tuesday was seven, and then usually by sleepy business travelers. Tonight, there wasn't a vacancy in the place. Clearly, the manager had only called her as a last minute resort. He probably wouldn't rest until after midnight, knowing then that she had finally punched out.

I helped raise two boys she thought to herself reassuringly, *I can handle seven more hours running this motel.*

As she settled into the idea somewhat assured, she saw Amy walking back towards her. The young woman leaned over the desk. "I almost forgot to tell you. We had a complaint from a guy who said the hot tub felt cool. It's no big deal really. We had a birthday party in the pool area earlier this afternoon, and the kids splashed a lot of water out. Ray filled it before he went home and said it's going to be a couple hours before it heats up to temperature. If anyone asks, just tell them that. It's most likely already warmed up, but I thought I should tell you."

Gretchen smiled and thanked Amy. She decided then that she liked the young woman and watched her jog back to her boyfriend who was now smoking a cigarette under the canopy. He ran his hand across his forehead, looked at his palm, and then wiped it on his sleeve. Amy opened the doors and joined him, and as they walked out from under the canopy, he said something to her, and they both looked up at the sun before walking out of sight.

The next hour slipped by very quietly. Gretchen finally resolved herself to watching guests go into the pool area. She was relieved when none came back out to complain about the hot tub. Now and then she looked out into the parking lot and could see a steamy haze rising from the car hoods.

Her first guest finally arrived. His hair looked damp. She ran his credit card through the machine while he stepped a few feet from the desk and opened a cellular phone. Though she tried not to, Gretchen listened.

"Hi. I just got in. The plane was a little late. Is everything okay?" He listened for a few seconds. "All right, we knew he was going to start talking back to you again, but we had talked about it. What did you do when he said that?" He listened for about thirty seconds, running his fingers heavily through his hair. "Ah Jesus, he walked away? What'd you say?"

Gretchen strained over the noise from the pool area to hear him.

"We talked about this, honey. You can't just do nothing. He's twelve. He's not going to start behaving better until he knows you mean business." He slipped his hand into his pocket and listened. He shook his head. "I'm two hundred miles away. You can't let him walk all over you. I'm just on the road too much right now."

Gretchen thought of how she and Joe had raised their boys. If the boys acted up during the day, she promised them swift punishment from their father that evening, which was no idle threat. This arrangement had worked out fine, but Gretchen couldn't imagine what she would have done had Joe been on the road for days or weeks at a time. She felt sorry for the woman on the phone.

"Are we done here? Can I go to my room?" the man asked, having caught Gretchen eavesdropping on his call.

Red-faced, she nodded and handed him his room key. Only after he had disappeared up the stairs did she notice that she hadn't had him sign his credit card receipt. Too embarrassed to call his room, she decided to wait to see if he would come back down. *He has to eat,* she thought.

While she tried to compose herself, the Abbots came out of their room wearing bathing suits. Gretchen noticed right away that Mrs. Abbot was heavy around the middle and bottom. *Why would she wear a bikini?* she thought. Although Mr. Abbot had a gut, his biceps looked like big potatoes. He tried to walk past the desk.

"Tell her," Mrs. Abbot hissed.

Mr. Abbot stopped and rubbed his face with his hands. "Christ, Tammy, I told you there's nothing they can do about it. The thing's blowing cold air . . ."

"No harm in telling her. We might get a discount. Just tell her."

Gretchen could hear them clearly, but tried not to stare. She looked out into the parking lot and saw a van pull in with large letters printed on the side. She made out the word COLLEGE.

When Mr. Abbot turned and stood at the front desk, Mrs. Abbot walked past him. "I'll be in the pool," she said loudly. "If they can't fix it, find out if we get a discount."

Mr. Abbot set his hands on the front desk and then pulled them back to rest at his sides.

"Is there a problem, sir?" Gretchen asked. She hoped it was something she could handle.

Mr. Abbot looked toward the closing pool door. "Not really," he said. "Our air conditioner is making a drumming sound, but it's working fine. I mean, it's blowing cold air."

"I could try to call someone in from maintenance," she said, but then remembered that her manager only wanted maintenance called in for emergencies.

"No, don't call anyone in. Thanks," Mr. Abbot said and walked towards the pool.

When he opened the door, the laughter and splashing grew louder for a moment. As the door closed, softening the noises again, Gretchen heard the dull thud of something hitting metal in the parking lot and looked outside.

Several big men in t-shirts were standing around the van that had just pulled in, and one was shaking the pain out of his right hand. After a few seconds, he stopped and examined his knuckles. They were all young men, maybe in their early twenties. She could see that the one with the hurt hand was the biggest of them, but they were all big with arm muscles like thighs. As they walked under the canopy, Gretchen saw that one had no bags, but carried instead two cases of beer.

When they came through the doors, Gretchen felt as though the lobby had shrunk. It seemed silly around them, like a dollhouse. The biggest of them was looking at his hand, and Gretchen could see that the knuckles were bleeding. Drawn to the sounds of the pool area, they walked over to the windows that looked in on the swimmers. One broke from the others and walked up to the front desk.

"We're part of the Cass College rugby team," he said, but didn't look at her, turning instead to watch his teammates.

Hoping that they were in the wrong motel, Gretchen flipped through the registry, but found that a registration had been made for six people from Cass College.

"Look at that fat ass," the biggest of them said. "How'd you like that on top?"

His words were followed by harsh whispers from the other players. Following their pointing fingers, he looked over at Gretchen.

"I don't give a shit," he said.

Gretchen avoided eye contact with the players and finished checking them into their rooms. The one at the desk handed her a check from the Cass College Accounting Office, and she handed him two keys. When she looked over at the other players again, she saw that the biggest was wrestling with another who finally fell back and knocked over a potted plant.

"Lighten up, you asshole," the one said, picking himself up.

"Come on, Jack, take it down a notch," another scolded.

The one at the front desk looked over and then held up the keys. "Let's go."

The other players began to pick up the luggage. Jack picked up the beer. "I'll take these," he said. "Let's go drink to our loss."

Gretchen tried to calm herself, but she was shaking. "You're right down there," she said and pointed them in the direction of the first floor hallway.

None of them thanked her. Their bodies rumbled past the desk like the eighteen-wheelers that always seemed about to edge her car off the highway. Another guest came down from the second floor, and Gretchen absently waved hello to him. He didn't wave back, and she realized, only after he'd left, that it was Charles Anderson, the man who still needed to sign his credit card receipt.

Before she could clean up the mess from the spilled plant, Gretchen had to check in the last guests for the evening, an older couple that was just walking in. They were about Gretchen's age, and she felt embarrassed by her uniform and name tag. The woman stood with her arm looped through her husband's. *That should have been Joe and I,* Gretchen thought after she handed them their key. To keep from crying, she scooped what soil she could back into the pot and then packed it down. Before vacuuming, she watered the plant, walking back and forth between it and the drinking fountain with a small plastic cup.

Mrs. Abbot came through the pool door as Gretchen was making her last pass with the vacuum. "Is anyone going to do anything about that hot tub?" she asked.

"What?" Gretchen asked.

"The hot tub is cold," Mrs. Abbot said angrily.

Gretchen remembered what Amy had told her and explained it to Mrs. Abbot. Half way through the explanation, Mrs. Abbot began to shake her head. She walked over to the pool door, opened it, and called to her husband. The door closed, and she looked at Gretchen.

The telephone rang.

"I have to go back behind the desk," Gretchen explained, but the phone stopped ringing by the time she got to it.

Mrs. Abbot opened the pool door again. "Get out here, Rick," she snapped.

After another thirty seconds, Mr. Abbot came through the door, his face long and angry. He walked with Mrs. Abbot over to the front desk.

"Tell her what you told me," Mrs. Abbot said.

"Ah, Christ . . ."

"Just tell her. She's trying to tell me that they put some new water in the hot tub this afternoon and that's why it's cold." As her husband started, she cut him off. "He used to clean pools as a business," she said.

"That water is really pretty cold, probably down a good ten degrees. I think your heater might be down," Mr. Abbot said. His wife smiled at him.

A hot sensation raced up Gretchen's spine. She looked at Mr. Abbot. "What do you think I should do?" she asked him.

Mrs. Abbot shook her head.

"Well," Mr. Abbot said, his voice deepening, "you need an accurate reading of the hot tub's temp. You got anything?"

Gretchen remembered that there was a thermometer on a thin rope behind the front desk. She bent, found it, and dangled it in the air for Mr. Abbot to see.

"Let's go check it out," Mr. Abbot said, walking toward the pool.

Gretchen followed him to the hot tub. Despite the cooler temperatures, a fat man was sitting in it, his hairy chest floating in the foam. Gretchen was embarrassed by his near nudity, but walked over and dipped the thermometer into the water.

"It is cool . . . tepid," the fat man said and then smiled agreeably to Mrs. Abbot.

"I know," Mrs. Abbot said. "We should complain to the manager tomorrow."

The fat man's kind smile dropped and he turned away to read the pool rules posted on a nearby wall. Mr. Abbot sat in a chair a few feet away rubbing his eyes with both palms.

While Gretchen waited for the reading, a man with a little girl on his shoulders waded from the deep end of the pool into the shallow end and then up the stairs.

"You might check the pool, too," he said, setting the girl on her feet. "It seems cold."

Gretchen could see the little girl's goose pimpled skin. "I will," Gretchen said. She felt alone, realizing more than ever that she was the only employee in the motel. When she pulled the thermometer out of the hot tub, she had trouble seeing the small numbers.

"Eighty-nine degrees," Mrs. Abbot, who had edged her way quite close to Gretchen, reported. "Isn't that low, honey?" she asked her husband.

"Sign on the wall says a hundred and one. Something's gotta be wrong for the temp to drop that low."

"What are you going to do?" Mrs. Abbot asked Gretchen. "We still have two more hours of swimming."

The thermometer slipped out of Gretchen's hands into the bubbling hot tub. The fat man reached down between his legs and handed it back to her. Gretchen suddenly felt as she had years ago when she had begun to have hot flashes. Forgetting to check the temperature of the pool, she walked out to the front desk. She thought she had told Mrs. Abbot that she'd call maintenance, but by the time she reached the pool door, she couldn't remember if she'd said anything to anyone. On the way out, she passed the rugby players who were on their way to the pool. She didn't look up at them.

She paged Tom Stanley, the maintenance man on call for that weekend. While she waited for him to return her call, she heard the rugby players begin yelling and swearing. Their voices echoed into the pool's high ceiling and drowned out the young laughter and shrills that had been there before. Soon after, guests began to leave the pool area, ushering children away from the profanity. Even with the closed door between the pool and front desk, Gretchen could hear each curse word clearly.

She was too nervous to talk to any of the guests leaving the pool area. She knew she couldn't do anything for them until maintenance arrived, so she unlocked the front desk manager's office and waited in the dark for Tom to answer the page. When he didn't, she paged him again. She heard pairs of wet feet flapping up to the front desk, stopping, and then flapping away. "Hello?" someone would call from time to time. *Just go to your rooms* Gretchen thought.

The phone finally rang, and she went back up to the front desk to answer it. She sighed in relief when she saw that no guests were waiting to complain to her about the rugby players. Tom was on the other end of the phone but, seeing the Abbots leaving the pool area, Gretchen asked him to hold, and she cupped her hand over the mouthpiece.

"I'm on the phone with maintenance right now," she said to them as they walked past the desk.

Mrs. Abbot didn't say anything, and Gretchen could see that she was crying.

"Honey, he wasn't saying that about you," Mr. Abbot whined. "I didn't really hear him say anything."

Mrs. Abbot stopped and wept into her palms, and Mr. Abbot put his arm around her, trying to cradle her head into his shoulder.

She slipped away from him. "I think you did hear him just fine," she said in between her shaking breaths.

"What do you mean?"

"I think you did hear him, and you knew he was talking about me," she said, her voice more controlled.

"Like hell. If what you're saying . . . I'm not afraid of them, Tammy. I'll go back in there right now if you want me to."

"Just come on," she said. She walked towards their room, her shoulders shaking again with sobbing.

Mr. Abbot caught up to her and put both arms around her. Her body seemed to collapse into his, and he guided her toward the room, speaking softly to her.

A few feet before they reached their door, Mrs Abbot said something and pushed Mr. Abbot away from her.

"Jesus Christ, honey," Mr. Abbot said, following her into the room.

After a few seconds Gretchen could hear a faraway voice coming through the receiver. "Hello?" she answered.

"Did you page me?" Tom asked angrily.

"Yes, I did." Gretchen said. She could hear a televised baseball game and the hum of an air conditioner from Tom's end of the phone. She explained everything to him about the hot tub. While she talked, she heard louder yelling coming from the pool. ("Don't be such a god damn asshole!")

Tom paused before saying anything. "Well, you'll need to make some signs that say 'pool out of order'. Tell the midnight person that I'll be in around six to look at the heater."

"Aren't you going to come in tonight?" Gretchen asked. She hoped he would come in so the rugby players would see him and know there was a man around.

"Nothing I could do tonight. Even if I got the heater running, it wouldn't make any difference to the water temp until after midnight."

"Maybe you could just come in and look at it. Maybe it would be easy to fix," Gretchen pleaded. She heard several men in the background shouting at something that had happened in the baseball game.

Tom exhaled loudly. "Are the pool lights on — you know the ones under water?"

Gretchen remembered that they were and told him.

"The pool lights are on the same breaker," Tom explained. "If the lights are on that means there's something electrical down on the heater . . . nothing easy to fix. Just hang the signs, and I'll be in in the morning."

Gretchen said good-bye and hung up the phone. She found paper behind the front desk and made the signs Tom had suggested. She was nervous for the next hour, but she saw no other guests going towards the pool. Outside of the yelling and swearing, everything seemed quiet. Gretchen took out some wood polish and sprayed down the front desk. While she rubbed it, she realized that she hadn't thought of Joe for some time. She decided that this more strenuous night was doing her some good. *Maybe I'll ask to work a few Saturdays in the future* she thought.

Ten minutes later, the door to the pool swung open and hit the wall.

"He is such a cock sucker," one of the boys was shouting. He walked with his head tipped back, his right hand pinching his nose. Watery blood ran down his face.

Another player was walking with him. "You know how he can get," he said as they walked past the desk.

"He's worse tonight."

They didn't look at Gretchen. A few yards behind them, the rest of the young men walked out circled around Jack. They were walking slowly.

"Not my fault he can't catch," Jack said. His hand was wrapped around a beer.

"Well, let's let him cool down a little. You threw that ball pretty hard," another of the players said.

"We decided it was first down, right? You get the ball back if your team gets first down, right? I was just giving him the ball."

"You whipped it right into his face."

"Alright, I'll say something to him."

Gretchen moved again after they passed.

An hour later, when several guests called in to the front desk, even some from the second floor, Gretchen knew what they were calling about. She'd been listening to the rugby players in their room from the front desk — yelling, cursing, arguing. A few times she'd heard a loud thud as though someone had hit a wall. They were as loud as they had been in the pool, and Gretchen had been sitting at the desk hoping they would tire out. Most of the guests on the phone were reasonable; they just wanted to know if she would call and ask the noisy room to quiet down. Every time she started to pick up the phone, however, she imagined and believed that their room was getting quieter. Then she'd wait.

The phone rang again, and Gretchen picked it up. "Front desk," she said.

"Are you deaf? Can you hear what they're doing in that room?" A woman asked, her voice slightly hysterical. "Just listen to them."

She must have taken the phone from her ear and set it near the wall because Gretchen could suddenly hear Jack's voice very clearly. ("And then the little faggot tells me that I won't pass his class.") She guessed the next sound she heard was a can of beer hitting the wall.

"This is Mrs. Abbot in room 107. We want to be moved."

Hopelessly, Gretchen flipped through the registry, knowing what she'd find before even looking. "I'm sorry Mrs. Abbot," she nearly whispered, "but all of our rooms are filled."

"Filled? Well you're going to have to do something."

Gretchen heard the word "something" shatter into sobs, and then Mrs. Abbott hung up the phone.

Gretchen knew what she'd have to do and finally made the call, taking a deep breath when the phone began to ring.

"Hello." It was Jack, and his voice sounded as though it were slipping out of his mouth before he intended it to.

"Yes, hello. This is the front desk calling." Gretchen paused and steadied her voice. "We've had a few complaints about the noise coming from your room."

"Hold on," Jack said.

Gretchen heard his palm scratching over the mouthpiece of the phone. She could still hear him laughing, and another voice came through the murmuring. ("Don't be a prick, man. She's probably someone's grandma.")

Jack came back on the phone. "I don't know what you're talking about. We're sleeping down here. You must have the wrong room."

Gretchen tried to harden her voice. "Sir, I know I have the right room."

"Look, goddammit, we're sleeping. Don't call here again. I don't come down there and bother you, do I? Do you want me to do that?" Jack asked.

("Come on, Jack.") someone in the room said.

Gretchen sat silently on her end of the phone.

"Don't call again," Jack finally said and hung up.

Gretchen remembered what the front desk manager had said about calling the police, how he'd explained that having them at the motel, especially at night, gave the place a bad name. "In a small town like ours, it can be fatal," he had said. "Try to handle all situations in-house unless it looks like someone is going to be hurt."

Remembering Jack's threatening words, she began looking for the police dispatcher's number. As she flipped through the telephone book she realized that the first floor was now silent. She waited, but only heard the hum of the air conditioning. *Maybe my call did quiet them down,* Gretchen thought. Nine minutes later, when she wheeled the mop and bucket of soapy water into the lobby, it was still peaceful. Relieved, Gretchen dragged the mop head back and forth across the floor. Her shift would be over in a half hour.

Feeling almost happy, she looked over at the potted plant the rugby players had knocked over earlier and could tell that it would live. Even the topmost leaves jutted out firmly on their stems. As she examined the plant, an unexpected idea came to her. *I could go to Hawaii by myself.* For a moment she tried to let the thought fade, but it remained, and she believed it. As though she were afraid she'd lose the impulse while sleeping that night, she walked quickly behind the front desk.

Trembling, she found a travel agent's number in the phone book. She wasn't surprised when nobody answered, but she left her own phone number on the agent's answering machine, along with a request to be called back. She was smiling when she hung up, excited by knowing that she'd set things in motion. She'd made a gesture that she could not withdraw. The travel agent would call her back Monday, would help her book a flight, reserve hotel rooms, plan sight seeing trips. In her excitement, she picked up a pen and forged Charles Anderson's signature onto his credit card receipt and then laughed to herself. It felt right to her to do something she'd never dared before.

Walking back from the mop room fifteen minutes later, she heard someone howling. Although she wasn't sure it was Jack, she knew that it was coming from the rugby players' rooms. She scurried behind the front desk to pick up the ringing phone. While she assured a guest that she was going to call the police, she saw Mr. Abbot coming out of his room wearing only his pajama bottoms. His hands were knotted into fists. Slamming his door, he started towards the front desk. His hair was matted in places and stuck up in others, and he looked as though he'd been suddenly woken. When he'd almost reached the spot where the carpeted hallway became the hard tile of the lobby, he stopped. Without looking at Gretchen, he turned around and stomped back to the rugby players' door. The report of his hand sounded like a hammer, and when they didn't answer, he started swearing at them. Then the door opened.

Trainee

Jeff Vande Zande

He always seemed to try to do everything very fast. When I started they had me on the Crustomatic for two days, flattening dough balls into crusts and then sticking the crusts into small, medium or large pans. But Gary, the owner's brother-in-law, was only on crusts for about two hours. "I have this down. What's next?" he asked Jim, the manager, who didn't have much choice but to show him what was next. By the end of the day he had already learned how to prep vegetables and take phone orders – things most of us didn't learn until the end of our first week. He was always asking, "What's next?" especially when the owner was around.

The owner had about twelve different Johnny Pizzas throughout northern Lower Michigan, and he'd brought his brother-in-law in to train him to be a manager for a store he was opening in Petoskey. None of us liked the owner very much because he lived in our town and spent a lot of time in our Johnny Pizza watching us. He was tall, bald, and the only person in town who had ever owned a Porsche. He always parked it out front, which was on the town's main drag, and I often saw people slow down to look at it.

Early on most of us didn't like Gary, the brother-in-law, but when he didn't try to act too much like a manager, we didn't like him or dislike him. He was just there, doing everything very fast, even when the place was slow.

Once, about a month after Gary started, I was watching him take pizzas out of the oven while I was on the phone with a customer. He snatched the pans with the metal tongs, edged the pizzas out with a spatula into the cardboard box, and zipped the cutter through—slicing smalls into eight pieces, mediums into ten, and larges into twelve. He was working like I'd seen Jim work on Friday nights when the pans would nearly back up because so many pizzas were coming through. Except Gary was only working the ovens on a Sunday lunch shift, and he had a good foot of space between pies. Still, he worked like we were in a rush, like everything was backed up. He had his tie tucked into his front pocket, and his shirt had crescent-moon sweat stains under the arms. The owner was on the phone next to me talking low to someone and watching everything.

I was about half way through the order when I saw how much Gary's face was sweating. He was leaning forward while slicing, and a bead of sweat dripped from his forehead, fell, and then splashed into the steamy sauce of the pizza under him. After a few seconds I realized I couldn't hear the owner's mumble anymore, and I guessed he was seeing what I was seeing. Gary kept working like he didn't know or like his sweat was just a free topping. And, it got worse – like two or three drops of sweat per pizza. The little red explosions mesmerized me. When I was just about through my order, I felt the owner next to me hanging up his phone. He took a long look out into the lobby, and when I followed his look, I saw that there weren't any customers waiting. He reached down to a shelf under the phones and then straightened, throwing a towel that hit Gary in the face. Gary jumped and then stood looking stupidly in our direction.

"Wipe your fucking face," the owner yelled. Back on the line, Chris and Tracy froze, their toppings dangling. They looked at each other and giggled. I don't know why, but I just felt sad watching this guy who was probably in his thirties rub a towel slowly over his face.

The next afternoon out back with Chris and me for a cigarette break, Sherri started telling us about how her older brother and his wife were moving out of Michigan to Texas to find work. She had a smudge of grease on her chest just under her right nipple, and I kept sneaking peeks at it.

It was the part of the shift I liked because we could take breaks while a few other people stayed in the store and handled the small number of orders. This was a good week since the owner was on the road doing inspections at his other stores. Even so, we all jumped a little when the back door opened and Gary stepped out.

He looked really tired, like the place had just been slammed, but we'd only had six orders in the last two hours. He sat down next to me on the picnic table, ran his hands through his thinning hair, and exhaled loudly. Sherri had stopped talking, and we were all taking quiet drags on our cigarettes, watching Gary. Like the rest of him, his face was soft, like dough.

He looked over at us, but at me more than anyone. "I used to smoke," he said and then loosened his tie. It was the first time he'd ever said anything to us. He'd asked us questions before about where we kept extra drums of sauce or how many pepperonis to put on a large, but he'd never *said* anything.

For a second nobody talked, and then I reached into my pocket, took out my pack, and shook one out for him. "You want one?" I asked.

He shook his head. "No, I quit four years ago. If I had even one I'd be back to a pack a day."

While he was finishing what he was saying, a rust-spotted car pulled into the parking lot and stopped about fifteen feet from us. A woman was driving it, and I could see one of those baby seats in the back. It seemed like she wanted to keep the car running, but the engine hesitated for a few seconds, hiccupped, and then stalled. She didn't restart it. Gary looked behind him at the car and then stood up.

"Ride's here," he said. "I'll see you all tomorrow."

He walked over to the car and the woman got out. She was a little overweight, but still pretty. We watched while Gary walked over to her and kissed her quickly on the lips. He went to a rear window, leaned, and waved like an idiot into the car. The woman, his wife I guessed, walked over to the passenger side and got in. After a second, Gary got in the driver's side, but he didn't start the car right away. I watched, and their lips moved, and he shook his head a lot. After a minute, his wife stopped talking and turned away towards her window. Gary started the car. Before he backed out, he looked over at us and saluted.

"That guy's such a loser," Chris said, lighting another cigarette. Chris was probably twenty-six and had worked at Johnny Pizza for about four years. I'd heard he'd once punched a dent into the door of the walk-in cooler.

"I don't know why," I said, "but I feel kind of sorry for him." Nobody said anything to that and eventually we started talking again until Jim leaned out the back door.

"I need someone to get in here," he said, "Kristen's late again."

Chris threw his cigarette at the door as it closed behind Jim. "Asshole," he hissed once the door closed.

A few days later the owner was back. I was up front working the cash register, counting my starting money for the dinner rush into the till, when Jim came in from the grocery across the street. The owner had this thing for expensive ice cream and was always sending Jim to buy him some. Jim always bought the ice cream with his own money, and sometimes the owner would pay him back and sometimes he wouldn't. Once in awhile I felt sorry for Jim because he seemed like a pretty decent guy.

I was counting the change into my till when the owner came up front, peeled the lid from his ice cream, and leaned into the counter. In between bites, he asked Jim questions about Gary. Gary wasn't in, but would be in a few hours to start a closing shift that would last until three or four in the morning. Because I was still in high school I didn't have to work closings, but I'd heard they were hell. One time after a party I drove by the store at about one in the morning. None of the big lights outside were on and the lobby was dark, but just beyond the counter I could see a few fluorescent lights. Someone was slowly pushing a mop back and forth, and it was one of the loneliest things I'd ever seen.

"How's he doing?" I heard the owner ask.

"Good," Jim said. "He's really got everything down pretty much—even most of the paperwork stuff."

"Does he do all right with the employees?" the owner asked after finishing a mouthful of ice cream.

"He seems to get along with everyone," Jim said.

The owner was quiet for a second. "No, I mean does he tell people what to do? He's so damn soft-spoken all of the time," he said.

I looked over at Jim as I finished with my starting cash and saw him work his left hand behind his head and rub his hair. He had short hair like he was in the army.

"He doesn't really say much to anyone," Jim said. "I mean, maybe he doesn't know he's supposed to."

"Doesn't know?" the owner said, kind of spitting out the words. "I'm training him to be a god damn manager. How the fuck couldn't he know that he has to tell people what to do?"

"I haven't said anything to him," Jim said. "I can tell him when he gets in - tell him that he's running the show for a few days."

The owner shook his head. "My sister can pick 'em," he said. "This Petoskey store is a big deal. I got a shit load of money sunk into it. I could have hired anybody, but I'm stuck with this guy, this . . ." His words trailed off.

"He'll be ready, I think," Jim said. "He's really smart, and he learns everything fast."

"I should hope he's smart," the owner said, smirking. He shoveled another scoop into his mouth.

I don't know if I was staring or not, but I saw the owner look over Jim's shoulder right at me. After a second Jim turned around.

"What are you doing, Terry?" he said, a little meanness in his voice.

"I just finished counting my starting cash," I said.

"All right, fine," Jim said and then looked towards the back of the store. "We look low on mediums. Go run about twenty-five crusts. You been here long enough to know that you need to find something to do when you're done with something."

I nodded.

"Then go do it!"

Asshole, I thought, as I headed to the back of the store. Dropping medium dough balls into the machine and watching them come out flat and stretched, I thought about quitting. I only had the job because my dad made me get one, and Jim had me feeling pretty puny. Maybe I would have even walked out, but Sherri started talking to me and I eventually forgot about it.

The next Friday when I came into the store, Jim put me on dishes right away so I could help Chris knock out the pizza pans that had piled up through a busy, under-staffed lunch.

"You hear what happened yesterday?" Chris asked, leaning his head down and pushing his glasses up with the side of his bicep.

I shook my head.

"Kristen came in about an hour late, and the owner was here, and he was pissed," Chris started. "He and Jim walked outside and talked for about ten minutes, and then Jim came back in and got Gary to go outside. I was working the cash register, so I could watch them. The owner did most of the talking, but Jim said a few things too, and Gary just stood there shaking his head a lot. After about five minutes the owner started yelling, but I could only hear that he was yelling, not what he was saying."

Chris stopped talking for a second while Jim cut through behind us.

"Come on guys," Jim said. "Ten more minutes on this. I need you to do other things, too."

We both nodded.

"Fuck you," Chris said when Jim turned the corner into the noise of the dough-making machine.

"What happened after the owner was done yelling?" I asked when Chris didn't start telling the story again.

"Oh yeah," he said, "anyway, the owner got in his car and made a big deal of squealing the tires as he pulled out. Jim talked with Gary for about another five minutes, and then the two of them came in again. Gary walked over to Kristen and took her off the pizza line and asked her to go into the office. She went along happily, you know how she is—not even a clue that she was about to get canned. Anyway, she was in the office with Gary for about ten minutes, and then she came out crying and ran out of the store. As soon as she was out the door, Jim went over to the time clock and dropped her card in. Gary didn't come out of the office for a long time, and when he did, he made crusts for about two hours and then left, even though he was supposed to stay until eleven."

I wanted to know more, but Jim came back, pulled me off dishes, and put me on crusts.

"Alright, I'll just stay here and wash dishes all damn night!" Chris yelled, slamming the pizza pans together.

Before I could start the crusts I had to go into the walk-in cooler to get some dough balls. I was a little surprised to see Gary leaning against one of the metal racks. In his hands he had a container of mozzarella cheese that he'd just refilled from the big cheese bins. His face looked really faraway and pale, like he'd just heard some bad news.

"You all right?" I asked.

"Yeah," Gary said, snapping to. "Just trying to remember what else I came in here for."

I knelt down and grabbed a tray of dough balls, and when I came back up with it he was gone.

About five hours later I was on break out back. It was about ten o'clock and it wasn't quite a spring night and it wasn't quite a summer night. It was cool but starry, and I was sitting on the picnic table enjoying my cigarette and enjoying the idea that my shift ended in an hour and a half. I knew where there was a party, and it was Friday, and everything seemed pretty good.

When I was into my second cigarette, the back door opened, and at first I just saw this dark silhouette in the harsh light glowing in the doorway. I guessed it was Jim coming to tell me to get back in, but when the door closed I saw Gary standing in the darkness.

"Terry?" he asked.

"Yeah," I said. I guessed that Jim had sent Gary out to come get me.

He walked over, climbed up onto the table, and sat next to me. He let his head drop back and he stared up into the sky. His face was shiny, and I could tell that he'd been sweating. I'd been on break long enough to even notice that he smelled like dough and grease – same way my mom always told me I smelled when I got home.

"Christ, it's a beautiful night," he said after a few seconds. "This reminds me of when I was in high school and I'd hang out on the beach at night with my friends. We'd just talk and talk about nothing all night."

I could feel him watching me for a moment.

"Let me bum a cigarette," he said, his voice like a kid's, a way I'd never heard it before.

I handed him my pack and he pulled one out. He put the cigarette in his mouth and turned the pack over in his hands for a few seconds. "Got a light?" he finally asked, handing the pack back to me.

I gave him my lighter. He lit the cigarette and took a long drag. Then he started coughing. "It's been a long time," he said, laughing. In a second he took another drag and exhaled slowly without coughing. "Man," he said, "my head's swimming." He slumped back onto his elbows and looked up at the sky.

"You think you're going to start smoking again, now?" I asked.

"No," he said, and took another drag. "But I miss it."

I twisted my cigarette out on the bottom of my shoe and started to get up.

"Terry, what year are you in school?" Gary asked.

"I'm a senior, but I graduate in a month or so."

"What are your plans after you graduate? You have something in mind?"

My father had put the same question to me the other night and I'd told him that I thought I'd go to the local community college. "Not really," I told Gary. "I think I'd like to take a year off."

Gary looked at me for a moment like he was thinking. "Nothing wrong with a year off."

"Yeah," I said, "I figure I can use that time to find out what I'd like to do."

"Yeah," Gary said, kind of laughing, "just make sure that what you like to do is also something someone would like you *to* do."

"What do you mean?"

"Do you like computers?" he asked.

"They're okay."

"Could you get to like computers? Could you see yourself getting to like computers enough to be a programmer? I mean, if you could, then there are people who would pay you good money. That's the trick, liking something that other people want to pay you to like."

I still wasn't sure what he was talking about. "I guess," I said.

Gary nodded and then laughed. "Whatever you do, don't get a goddamn degree in history."

"All right," I said, kind of laughing myself, "I won't."

"Good," Gary said. He took a few drags on his cigarette and eventually blew a smoke ring. It floated above us briefly and then faded into the darkness.

"Can I ask you something?" I said.

"Go ahead."

"Why do you go so fast all of the time? I mean, even if we're slow you go really fast."

Gary pinched his nose a few times between his thumb and finger and looked thoughtful. "I guess I'm just trying to get out of here. I can't stand that asshole. I figure if I can show him that I can do it, then I'll get to Petoskey all the sooner."

I nodded.

"Even though it looks like now he's going to keep me here for another month at least. He's going to open and manage the Petoskey store himself until he feels I'm ready. That's where he is now — over in Petoskey hiring and training the new crew — my crew. He didn't even take me with him."

"That's bull," I said after a few seconds. "Why don't you quit?"

"I should," Gary said, as much to himself as to me. "I can't tell you how much I hate this place, and he . . ." He stopped short.

The back door swung open. I could tell by the buzz cut on the silhouette that it was Jim staring into the darkness at us.

"Come on guys, I need you back inside," Jim's voice said.

I started to move, but I felt Gary's hand grab my arm. "We're going to take another minute," he said. "Terry and I have been killing ourselves in there, and we just need to slow down."

"What? We're all killing our . . ." Jim started. Then I guessed he realized that he was talking to the owner's brother-in-law. He stood in the doorway for a few seconds. "All right, but not too long."

"Hey Jim? We'll come in when we're ready," Gary said.

Jim stepped back into the store and let the door close behind him.

I'd never really heard anyone talk to Jim that way except for the owner. I looked over at Gary and could tell that he was smiling.

"Let me have another smoke," he said.

I shook one out of the pack for him, and when he put it in his mouth I lit it. Then I lit one for myself and joined him as he lay back on the table looking up into the thousands of stars.

"Hey, you want to go to a party?" I asked after a few minutes. "I mean, some college guys are throwing it, so there'll be some older people there, too."

Gary exhaled loudly for nearly five seconds, like he was trying to blow out a trick candle. When he sat up, I sat up with him waiting to see what he was going to do next. I half suspected that he might walk out that night, and if he wanted to leave right then I was ready to go with him.

Standing, Gary flicked the spent butt of his cigarette towards the parking lot where it exploded into sparks and then disappeared.

"Come on," he said, "let's get back in there."

I watched him walk over to the door and open it. He then disappeared into the blinding fluorescence. Last I heard he was managing the Johnny Pizza in Petoskey. As it turned out, the owner and his wife moved there, too.

I didn't follow him back into the store. I left my Johnny Pizza hat and my Johnny Pizza shirt on the picnic table and drove back to my parents' house to shower before the party. While driving home I thought about Gary and tried to imagine him still at the store with his hands full of mozzarella cheese or dealing pepperonis onto a pie. Picturing it started to get me kind of sad.

Tired of thinking about him, I started thinking about the party instead. I wondered if there would be any good-looking girls there. Lately I'd been thinking that I should have a girlfriend, some kind of relationship in my life.

Jeff Vande Zande

Downstream Water

Jeff Vande Zande

He could feel the weight of the nightcrawler as it sailed through the air pulling line off his reel. For a few seconds the only thing he knew in the world was its brief flight. It was a good cast, just enough snap in his wrist to land the bait upstream from the dark pool, where it would tumble in naturally like any feed in the river. Pulling his arm back, he'd stopped the cast short, leaving slack so the worm would slide into the hole at the speed of the current. He could feel the heavy rush of water behind him working at his legs. In most places the river moved leisurely, but here, about thirty yards below a mild run of rapids, the pushing was more insistent, and he struggled at times to keep his balance. A sound exploded from his creel like a hand swiped back and forth across a wicker chair, and he felt the thumping of a brown trout he'd caught earlier that afternoon as it thrashed in its dying. He looked down through the hole, but couldn't see the fish in the blackness.

Soon he felt a slight tug at the end of his line as it finally pulled taut with the weight of the nightcrawler. While reeling in the bait, he wondered if the large hole was worth another cast. Over the past few months he'd learned that most holes on the Black, no matter what the size, usually hit on the first cast, or they didn't. He didn't like that kind of fishing. It seemed to lack sport or any sense of finesse. In his youth he had fished the Yellow Dog and remembered picking up trout on the third or fourth cast into a hole, sometimes enticing a three or four pounder out of the safe shadows of a log. There was a mystery to that kind of fishing that he enjoyed. He remembered that his father, a fly fisherman, had always said that the fishing, not the fish, was the important part. It was now, at thirty-seven years old, that he was starting to understand what his father had meant.

Charmed by the eddy of hazy images from his youth, he decided he'd hit the hole one more time. His legs were tired from fighting the strong current, and he knew that stretches downstream held promising cover, but he was determined, despite even his loneliness, to continue rethinking things, to go against what common sense told him—try to avoid its common results.

Before casting again, he gave any fish that might be in the hole a moment to settle, just in case the first cast and retrieve had spooked them. Standing in the river, he had a moment to look around him, a moment to breathe and think about nothing. He looked ahead to read the river, but already knew this stretch's riffles, pools, submerged rocks, and deadfalls. He looked away from the water. Along the banks he watched the wind ruffle the long grass and rock the black spruce and swamp hardwood rooted in stands a few yards in from the river. On a tree close to the bank he spotted a chickadee as it flitted from branch to branch. It looked around, and its head jerked and twitched in a frenzied pivot. When he tried, he could even hear the slight fluttering from its tiny wings.

Something rustled on the left bank, and he turned just in time to see the slick fur of an otter slip into the water. Its head emerged briefly about fifty feet downstream and then dropped into a pool around the base of a fallen jack pine. He closed his eyes and imagined the otter's dive into the hole, could feel the tickle as it slid down through the web of roots. Holding there along the bottom, deep in the shadows, brown trout intermittently snapped their strong tails against the current. He felt himself becoming the otter, moving quickly, hugging his claws into the spine and underbelly of a fish, biting it around the base of its head to stop the heavy thrashing. He stood in the river—eyes closed, mouth open—feeling his jaw stretch around the fish's thick body. He felt the thoughtless joy of knowing hunger would soon end, the blood and bone happiness of satisfying the most basic appetite, if only for a few hours. He dragged his prey into the wet grasses along the bank, flanked himself within the safety of some mud hole, and bit through the fish and into the pink meat.

A few seconds after he opened his eyes, he saw the otter itself surface again further downstream. Its mouth was empty. He watched it as it moved along with the current. Eventually its head slipped under again and, though he waited it, he did not see it come up. Scanning the surface, he saw a fish rise and remembered why he was standing in the river.

He cast his bait upstream from the hole he had fished earlier. For a few seconds it tumbled with the current, but then his pole bent with the weight of something heavier than just the sinkers and worm. He lifted the tip high, setting the hook, and waited to feel what the fish was going to do. Its first effort was to swim hard across the river toward the deeper water of an undercut bank, and he could tell from its strength that it was not a very big fish. Still, with a potato and a hunk of bread it would make a meal. Knowing that the test of his line was stronger than the fish, he simply reeled it in. Before long he was holding it, a rainbow trout a little over ten inches long. Its writhing weight felt good in his hand. Slipping the fish into the dark creel, he heard it begin its mad thrashing. The other fish did nothing and he knew that it was dead or would be soon. He looked downstream momentarily but then decided he had enough fish. He knew that he really didn't have any place cool to keep a larger haul anyway. Turning, he began the slow wade back to the cabin.

Where he could he made his way to the bank and out of the water to avoid walking against the current. Most of the waterfront property was owned along this stretch of the river, but he knew nobody was here to accuse him of trespassing. He studied the small, knotty pine cabins and walked leisurely across the manicured grass, knowing that the owners were probably working somewhere in Detroit or Pontiac or Flint. This weekend they'd be here, bringing the sounds of the suburbs with them—the laughter of children, barking dogs, the drone of lawnmowers. Sometimes, in the evening, he even heard the sound of canned television laughter drifting through an open window. He'd learned over the last couple months to stay around his cabin on the weekends, working in the garden or fixing things. There was always the huge tree trunk he was slowly hollowing into a canoe. Whatever he did, he tried to remember that the disturbance would only be for a couple days. Late Sunday afternoons he'd hear the cars fire up, fathers holler for children and dogs, doors slam, gravel spit out from under tires. Then he'd know everything was his again.

It wasn't that he hated people. He simply felt that talking to anyone might stop what he had started to discover —might take him off track. And he knew it wasn't good for a lot of people to see him anyway. He was pretty sure people were looking by now.

A thick stand of trees grew on either side of the river just before his cabin. In the past he had tried to push his way through, but the heavy undergrowth slowed him, and hidden branches came close to puncturing his waders. Though tired, he eased his way back into the river and worked against the crotch-high current. The walking burned in his upper thighs, but within a few minutes he could see his property. When he looked towards his cabin, he was startled to see a woman watching him from the bank. She was wearing a blazer and business skirt and, holding its handle with both hands, she dangled a briefcase against the front of her thighs. He continued to walk and studied her as he did. She was thin, but not skinny, and he could tell, even from twenty-five yards away, that he would find her pretty. Her blonde hair was pulled up into a loose bun. Though he had imagined many times what this meeting might be like, he had never pictured that they would send a woman, especially not an attractive one.

"Mr. Carter?" she asked, when he was about ten yards away.

"Yeah," he said. It was the first word he had spoken in three weeks, and his hoarse voice sounded different to him, older.

She just nodded and then watched him make his way out of the river. The bank in front of his property was undercut and deep.

"Just give me a second," he said and then set his pole up on the grass. He planted both palms on the bank to try to push himself up from the river. On his first attempt, his arms eventually buckled and he sank back down. "Goddammit," hissed from between his teeth.

The woman passed her briefcase into her left hand and took a step forward.

"I've got it," he said. He crouched as low as he could without getting water inside his waders. After a few seconds of breathing he jumped while pushing and was eventually able to struggle his left leg onto the grass. With the added leverage he was able to hoist the other up and then roll over. She looked down and smiled at him. He guessed she was in her early thirties.

"Not usually someone here when I do that," he said after a heavy breath. He sat up, knelt, and then stood.

"Maybe you could use a ladder or a rope?" she said. She pushed a few strands of hair away from her eyes.

He looked at her and then at the bank. "Maybe," he said. "Wouldn't take much to build one." He looked back at her and then her briefcase. "Maybe not."

She seemed to know what he was thinking. "I'm June Thorpe," she said and held out her right hand, "from Lenders One?"

He nodded and took her sweaty palm.

"They just sent me out here . . . just to look at things. I'm just making sure there hasn't been any storm damage. I didn't think you'd be here. You are *Stanley Carter*."

"Yeah. Well, Stan," he said. He remembered that about a month ago some high winds had whipped through the area knocking down trees. One cabin about a mile downstream had lost part of its roof. Looking at her briefcase Stan didn't feel ready to hear what else he knew June would say. "I got to clean these fish," he said. He saw her nod, and then he knelt and unbuckled the leather strap on top of the creel. Opening it, he took out the brown trout. It was dead, but not quite stiff yet.

"Why is there grass in there?" she asked.

He stuck the end of a filet knife down near the fish's anus and then slit it up to its gills. "Keeps the creel cool," he said. He used his finger to scoop out the guts. After about a minute he started the other fish. He looked up at her once, thinking she'd be looking over his property, but she was watching him closely, especially his face. He tried not to think about what her arrival meant.

"You're good at that," she said as he finished the second fish.

"Not much to it," he said. With each thumb inside a fish where the guts had been he wrapped the rest of his fingers around their spines and leaned over the bank to swish them clean in the water.

"The company has sent a lot of mail," she said behind him. "They left messages on your machine . . . until your phone was disconnected."

"I imagine," he said, getting back to his feet. "Let's go up on the porch so I can get these waders off." He could feel her following him. He stopped at the edge of the small garden he had dug and tilled a few months ago. Already the green tops of vegetables stood anywhere from one to five inches above the soil.

"Have you had anything out of there, yet?" she asked.

"Radishes," he said.

"I love gardens," she said, her voice full of sighs.

He nodded and then started walking toward the porch again. Once up the steps, he shrugged off his suspenders and began to push down his waders. She was on the second step, watching him. "Sit down," he said and motioned with his head toward the rocking chair.

"I don't have everything here," she said. "I can't tell you everything. I don't think they thought I'd bump into you here."

He hung his waders on a peg and smiled. "Where do they think I am?"

"I haven't heard too many people talk about you, really. I talked to my boss a little bit before I came out, and he said you were probably dead, probably that they'd find you in some dumpster eventually. I'm really just out here to assess the property."

"You saw me in the river?" He sat down on the top step of the porch.

"Yes. I was looking around, and I could tell *someone* was living here. Then I heard you in the water." She looked at him. "I thought those things kept you dry," she said, and looked at his pants.

He looked too and could see the wetness in his jeans. "Sweat," he said. When he looked at her, he could feel himself looking at places other than her eyes. Thinking how long it had been since he'd been with a woman helped him not think about what he didn't want to think. "I guessed someone would eventually come out to talk to me," he said, looking toward the river.

"Why are you here?" she asked after a few seconds.

He snickered and didn't say anything for a moment. Though he was interested in her, especially for her questions, he knew why she had come. "We don't have to do *this*. Just open up the briefcase. I'll sign what I need to sign."

"No, I really want to know. I don't have anything for you to sign," she said. Her voice sounded genuine and pleading.

He looked at her and thought he saw something in the way her eyes studied his face. She seemed to want to see something there, and when their eyes met, he had to turn away back toward the river. He ran his fingers into his curly beard, scratching at some ingrown hair, and then remembered how long and shaggy his hair had looked that morning in the mirror. If she was looking at him intently, it must have only been out of curiosity he decided. "I guess I don't know why I'm here," he said.

"How long have you been here?" she asked.

"Three months," he said.

"Are you okay? I mean, do you feel all right?" she asked.

"I'm not out of my head," he said. He could tell now by the way that she looked at him that she was attracted to him. He'd been told that he was handsome – that he had a rugged face.

"Don't think you have to soften me up. I know what I did. Just say what you have to say."

She was quiet for a minute. "You defaulted. The bank will foreclose. Sell everything. This place, your house down in Farmington. That's what they do. I mean, they have to." Her voice seemed to rise, almost sounded frustrated, but not angry.

"I imagine," he said, looking back toward the river. "Can't really blame them." He was quiet. He didn't feel that there was anymore to say.

"I still want to know though . . . I mean why you came here," she said after nearly a minute. Her voice was soft, almost ghostly.

He looked back at her, and they looked into each other's eyes. He didn't look away. "Want a little whiskey?" he asked after a few seconds.

"No," she said. "Do you have anything weaker?"

"Whiskey and water."

She shrugged and then nodded. "I'll take lots of water, though."

He went into the cabin while she waited on the porch. As he poured the drinks, he wondered where he would live after the foreclosure. *How will I live?* He knew everything was coming to an end. His tumbler was nearly half full, but he swallowed it like a shot and then refilled it.

Stepping back out onto the porch, he handed her a drink that looked similar to the golden color the river became as it reflected its sandy bed. His own was darker, more the color of the bottom itself.

"This isn't bad . . . just a little sting," she said, after a cautious sip. Then she took a longer drink and coughed.

"You don't have to drink it," he said, laughing.

"No, it's good," she said, taking another sip. Then she set the drink down, stood, and slipped off her blazer. She looked at him and motioned towards the rocking chair.

He didn't say anything for a second. "Oh, no go ahead," he said. "I'm fine here." He knew that she had seen where he was looking – that he wasn't looking at her face. Flustered, he sat down on the top of the steps.

"It's really beautiful out here," she said. "My fiancé . . . well, my ex-fiancé has a place like this on the Manistee."

He nodded, but looked out toward the water again. Taking drinks from his whiskey, he tried to find a way to begin. Across the river a hornet's nest the size of a basketball dangled from a thin branch above the water. It seemed impossible, a defiance of gravity. Even from thirty yards away he could see the insects flying into and coming out from the hole. "I can't make any sense of it – not in words," he finally said.

"What did you do? I mean, where did you work before this?" she asked.

He looked at her and smiled and then looked at her briefcase. "You don't already know? My life story's on that damn mortgage application."

"I didn't read it," she said. "I don't really know anything about you other than your residences. I drove over here from Gaylord because the Detroit office asked someone from our office to check the place out. It's not like you're on my caseload or something," she said, her voice growing higher in pitch.

"Alright, alright," he said. "I worked at an engine assembly plant in Novi."

"Did you hate it or something?" she asked, her voice relaxed again.

"Not like some guys do. I didn't really like it, but it paid good—I liked it for that. It bought me this place. Almost." He took another drink. "You see that? Fish jumped. Nice one, too."

She leaned out toward the water, but then shook her head.

"Always loved this place," he said, his voice almost dreamy. "Came here every two-week vacation and most weekends in the summer, and I'd almost cry when we had to go back."

"We?"

"My wife and daughter," he said. He tilted his head and glass and finished his whiskey. Then he stood. "Lost them three years ago. Coming back from the dentist, hit a patch of black ice on I-696 . . . went over the guardrail."

"Oh, I'm so sorry," she said and looked as though she would stand.

Before she could he slipped through the screen door and back into the dark cabin. When he came out, tumbler refilled, he saw that she had moved and was now sitting on the top step. "You can see the river better from here," she said. "I think I saw a fish jump."

If he hadn't been drinking, he'd have sat in the rocking chair, but the whiskey had him feeling good, and he knew that she liked him. When he sat down next to her he saw that she'd rolled her sleeves and pulled the bottom of her blouse out of her skirt. They both watched the river, though he was more aware that their hips were touching and she wasn't moving away. "Don't be so quiet," he said after a minute. "I can talk about it now."

"It's just so sad," she said.

"Yeah, it was really sad. Probably part of the reason I'm here now. I mean, after the funeral I *did* go back to work. For three years I kept on the same way, as though they were still alive. I didn't really know anything else."

They were quiet again for nearly a minute. A diverse sound of birds came in from the trees — inharmonious, but not ugly, like a symphony tuning and warming up their instruments.

Stan stared across the river into the tree trunks that staggered back into the eventual darkness. He wanted to finish the thoughts he had started. "I wasn't thinking about them when I walked out of work that day," he said. "It was something that built up. On a Monday I looked down and I couldn't believe my hands were mine, like I was watching someone else's hands. I worked that way for three days, kinda outside of myself, and then on Thursday I couldn't take it anymore and I walked. Just felt empty. You know what I mean?"

"I think I've felt like that in the morning," she said. "I'll see my face in the mirror, but I have a hard time believing that I'm real. It's scary."

He nodded. "I had to get out, so I jumped in my car and drove here." He looked over at her and could see that she was taking her last drink. He watched her lips on the rim of the glass. She coughed again when she pulled the glass away.

"What will you do now?" she asked after clearing a tickle in her throat.

"Don't know. When I was a husband and father, I knew what to do. I kind of miss that . . . you know, knowing what to do. Even then, though, something wasn't quite right. I see that now. It wasn't them . . . my wife and daughter. I mean, I loved them. It's more like something was missing sometimes in me, or I was missing something. I don't know. It's just that now I'm just finding out each day what I need to do. And, whatever it is I'm doing, I like it . . . everything about it. Most of the time. Other times I feel like I'm nuts."

"I couldn't do it," June said, looking into her empty glass. "I'm scared to be alone. I don't even like being in my apartment by myself."

Stan took another sip of his own drink and could feel himself loosening. He looked over at June. "Do you want another?" he asked.

She smiled. "No thanks. I really have to get back to the office. I think I've already been here too long."

"No," Stan said. It was the first time in many months that he felt he needed to be with someone. "You have to stay," he said, smiling. "You have to explain everything that's going to happen . . . I mean with the bank."

"There's really nothing to explain . . ." June started, seriously.

"Well, just stay then . . . just for dinner. I'll cook those fish." He looked into her eyes and neither looked away.

"All right," she said, smiling. "Let's eat those fish."

He told her where the pantry was and said she should pick out whatever vegetable she wanted with the meal. When she came back her arms were full of corn. "I love corn. My dad used to stop at roadside stands all the time when I was a little girl," she explained excitedly. "He always seemed his happiest when he had a passenger seat full of sweet corn."

Stan made a fire in the pit because the electric company had long since turned off his power.

"You spend the night out here in the pitch black?" she asked.

"The dark's not scary."

In the fading light of the day, she fussed with the ears of corn, pulling each stringy strand from between the kernels as she shucked. Stan set the filets in a frying pan with butter and pepper and worked them over a small alcove of hot coals. He looked over towards his half-finished canoe up on sawhorses and realized that it was more tree than boat. He tried not to think about what was ending or where he would go from here. Taking sips from his whiskey helped him not to think.

"You have a pot for these?" she asked, holding the yellow ears out toward him.

"Inside. Above the sink," he said.

"Are you okay?"

"Fine," he said. He tried to smile some of the tension out of his face.

"This is fun," she said. "I feel like Laura Ingalls or something."

"It's great, isn't it?"

"It's nice for a change – a nice getaway," she said before stepping lightly up the stairs, across the porch, and into the cabin.

He felt happy as he listened to the fish sizzling.

After dinner they sat on the porch as dusk darkened towards night. June sat in the rocking chair and Stan sat on the top step. Each time he looked back at June more of the details of her face were faded into silhouette.

"What *are* you going to do now?" she asked.

She'd asked the question he'd been trying not to ask himself ever since she'd showed up. "Don't know," he said.

"Could you go back to the plant?"

"Christ no, and I wouldn't want to," he said. He stood, went back into the cabin, and poured himself another whiskey. He hoped she'd stop talking about his plans because he didn't have any. He was starting to wish that he wouldn't have asked her to stay.

He went back out to the porch and leaned against the wall. He tried to listen for the churn of the river, but June started talking again.

"Would you think of working up here somewhere?" she asked.

"Really don't know. Haven't thought about it." He took a long drink from his whiskey. "Have you ever swam at night?" he asked, suddenly.

"No!" she said.

"I do it every night. The river's cold, but there's a hole right in front of the cabin here where the current seems to slow down a bit." The idea of swimming with someone excited him.

"I'm not swimming in the dark. I don't even have a swim suit," she said.

"You don't need a suit."

She was quiet for a few seconds. "I'm not going to swim."

"Well, all right, just come down to the river and watch me then," he said.

She didn't say anything, but eventually stood and followed him off the porch. "I can't even see where I'm going," she said after a few seconds.

Stan turned around, took her hand, and led her down to the water.

The river was moving blackness, and its murmur was louder than it was during the day.

"I can't believe you're going to swim in there," she said.

"Well, I am," he said. He began to strip down.

"God, you could give me some warning," June said. She turned away.

Stan apologized. He set his clothes in a neat pile and then jumped about three feet out from the bank into the water. Setting his feet down, he rooted himself into the river bottom and was able to stand.

"It's so buggy," she said.

Stan could see her silhouette and was glad when she finally crouched and then sat on the bank. A light snow of insects was playing on the surface of the river. "I think they're white mayflies," he said. "This could even be a small hatch. You know, they live under water for about three years . . . only fly for a day or two. Most of these will be dead by tomorrow. They don't bite though, not like mosquitoes."

"Something on shore is biting," she said and then slapped her neck.

Stan let his legs drift up and then did a crawl against the current. After two minutes, he'd made no progress upstream but hadn't been pushed downstream at all either. He was breathing hard when he stopped. Looking over at her, he was happy to see that June was dangling her feet over the bank and into the water, although her hands were busy brushing bugs from her face and slapping them from her arms and neck. He stood in the river letting the water work around him.

"I could help you, you know," she said. "I mean with the bank."

"What?"

"You don't have to lose everything. There are people I can talk to. I mean, the banks don't want to foreclose. Better for them if everyone just goes on paying their interest. You don't really want to lose your house," she said.

And to keep from doing that, he knew what he'd have to do. To hold onto the large house he owned and pay the property taxes, he'd need to work—in the strictest sense. The kind of work that they pay you for, and the only reason that you do it is because they pay you for it. The kind of work that you contort your hands and mind into to make them fit. It seemed ugly to him now, selling hours of his life. No money was worth it. He couldn't go back, not feeling what he now felt.

"You wouldn't want to lose this place, would you? I mean, you're going to have to do something." She spoke quietly, but loud enough to be heard above the river.

Stan felt the cold of the river starting to numb his body since he had stopped moving. Nothing was left from the whiskey. She was saying what he'd refused to let the voice in his head say. She was asking the questions he didn't want to answer. In the short time he knew her, he already liked her; the fact that she stayed out here with him for dinner and asked him questions suggested that there was something to her.

He couldn't blame her for asking him what he planned to do. But, as he thought about it, he really had no idea what he wanted, no idea what he would do. If he left now, he knew he'd never get back to the place he had arrived in the last three months. If he tried to stay, the bank would foreclose and he'd be forcibly removed from the property. Either way, he would lose all of the new feelings. If he did go back to some kind of work, he could still come here during two-week vacations and on weekends. *That wouldn't be enough anymore* he thought. Standing quietly in the river he felt himself shivering, not only with cold but with something bigger than cold. He felt cornered.

"Stan?" she asked.

Without thinking anymore, he turned, dove, and swam underwater with the current. He knew the river here, knew that there was nothing for him to run into as he moved smoothly with the dark water. His lungs burned as he tried to stay under for as long as he could. When he surfaced he was about two hundred yards downstream. The moon glowed brightly, and he could see thousands of insects — nymphs unfolding at the surface into wings. He wasn't sure if June could see him, or if his head just looked like flotsam, but she screamed his name. He didn't answer, and the current eventually swept him out of the luminescence and into the blackness of a bend in the river.

Reception

Jeff Vande Zande

In the dim light of the reception hall Catherine became aware of Michael, her husband, striding towards her. His feet kicked up dead leaves as he walked. From the darkness of a corner table, she had been scrutinizing Bobby, her new son-in-law, as he talked with someone from his side of the family near the bar. The tiny ember of his cigarette flitted in the air, and she guessed he was telling some asinine story. It was the most she'd ever seen him talk. *I really don't know him at all*, Catherine thought, shaking her head. She still couldn't understand why Theresa wanted to marry him — a short, skinny house painter. Catherine didn't believe he'd ever start the contracting company he sometimes made claims about. The way he talked about the business reminded her of her father and the way he had always talked about saving enough money to move the family out of Redford into nearby Farmington Hills. Despite his talk, her father still lived in the same small three-bedroom he had purchased when he'd first started on the line at Ford.

The dinner had ended over an hour ago and now guests were moving about and talking. The DJ played slower music so couples could dance. Catherine watched one of the groomsmen dip his girlfriend ludicrously close to the floor and then sweep her back up. They laughed. Catherine shook her head and turned away. Looking at the assortment of crooked gourds and tiny pumpkins in the centerpiece of the table didn't help her mood. She couldn't believe she'd let Theresa talk her into these decorations. Throughout the room were corn stalks, cornucopias, garlands of dried roses and dried hydrangea, grapevine wreaths, and arrangements of chrysanthemums, carnations, and Peruvian lilies. Where the light was bright, the room was washed in yellow, orange, bronze, and maroon. Most of it seemed so melancholy, but also fitting for what Catherine guessed would almost certainly end in divorce. This October wedding wasn't at all the summer affair she had always imagined for her only daughter.

When he reached the table, Michael looked winded, sweaty — the way he looked when he came home from one of his infrequent racquetball games. Leaves crackled under his feet.

"I told her the leaves would get spread all over the place," Catherine said. Shaking her head, she regarded Michael's pinecone boutonnière.

"Troy is here," Michael sighed.

"What? Inside? He's in the reception hall?" The news ran hotly along her spine. She had not thought of Theresa's old boyfriend in over a year.

"No, he's not inside . . . not yet," Michael said. He pulled out a chair and lowered himself into it.

"Where is he, Michael?" Catherine asked, frustrated that she always had to prod him with questions to get an entire story.

"He's across the street in the parking lot near the baseball field. He's just sitting on the hood of his car." Michael rubbed his left eye.

Despite his height and his executive position at Chrysler, Catherine's husband seemed small to her, defeated. "How did you find out he was here?" she asked.

"I heard one of Theresa's old college friends say he was out there. I went out and talked to him. I told him this was really inappropriate." Michael pushed both hands through his gray hair.

"What did he say?"

"He told me to . . . well, he just didn't leave. He's still here," Michael said. His hands flipped around like leaves. The gesture made Catherine feel sorry for him. She knew he had tried everything he could with Troy. At one time it even seemed like the young man was out of their lives. Reaching across the table, she set her hand on top of both of his.

Theresa had met Troy during her sophomore year at the University of Michigan. He was only a freshman then, but he was a second stringer on the football team and a major in business. They'd become serious very quickly Catherine remembered. Later Theresa would say that she only loved him because he seemed like everything she was supposed to love. Years ago, Troy was the man Catherine wished would have married her daughter. Early on Catherine sensed that he would do whatever it took to get what he wanted.

A song she'd heard many times before at wedding receptions started to play, and Catherine shook her head. She'd never understood why it was so popular. As she watched some of her friends leave the dance floor, she saw the groomsmen spill onto it and form a small eddy of tuxedoes. Laughing, they thrashed their arms around and swung their hips from side to side. Leaves flipped up around their feet.

Close friends of Catherine and Michael stopped by to say that everything was lovely. Catherine and Michael smiled and then thanked them.

"I really don't know if we need to do anything about it. He's just sitting on his car," Michael said after the couple stepped away. He pushed his chair so it teetered on its back two legs.

Catherine watched the groomsmen. Eventually the lyrics "ride your pony" began to repeat, and one of the groomsmen swung a leg up over an imaginary horse and grabbed an invisible rein. He began to trot his feet. *Unbelievable*, Catherine thought. She knew these were the men Theresa would know for the rest of her life. They reminded her of the men in the neighborhood she had grown up in—struggling men who lived in small houses with old cars and small yards. They were the same men Catherine had wished weren't her neighbors when she was a teenager. Considering the groomsmen, Catherine felt sad for Theresa. Even with her job at the D.I.A. these men would still be in her life, keeping her from more influential acquaintances.

Michael set his chair back down on all fours and stood up. "I really don't think he'll do anything," he said. "He won't come in." He walked away toward the bar.

Thinking of Troy again took Catherine out of her sadness into something closer to fear. She wasn't sure what Troy might do.

* * *

Theresa had broken up with Troy right after he'd ambushed another student outside of an apartment building and busted his jaw. Theresa had been studying with the other student for an upper division literature course she was taking. Troy had told her several times to stop studying with him, but she needed the class to graduate, so she ignored his jealousy. Theresa told Catherine that she'd never really guessed that Troy could be so violent. Before that incident, he had been possessive, telling her who she should have as friends and what parties she couldn't go to, but he had never given any indication that he would hurt someone over her. He spent the rest of the semester tangled up with lawyers, and Theresa saw very little of him. Now and again he left messages on her answering machine that said he still wanted to be with her. She later heard that he'd dropped out of school to take a position working for his father's chain of office supply stores in Detroit. Not long after, Theresa graduated and moved back home, not surprisingly to Catherine, who had always doubted the value of an Art History major. Once Theresa was back home, the trouble with Troy really began.

At first he only called infrequently to see how Theresa was doing. Then he started calling every day. "No, Troy. No, it's just not going to happen," Catherine remembered Theresa often saying from her end of the phone. "Because I know you won't change, that's why." Catherine had even considered telling Theresa to give the boy another chance, but a few weeks later he stopped calling. Soon after, someone began to call the house at different times throughout the day and hung up whenever someone answered. Then calls began to wake the house late at night, sometimes as late as two or three o'clock in the morning. If anyone other than Theresa answered, the caller hung up. When she did answer, whoever was on the other end just listened. "Troy, I know this is you," Theresa would say. "You better stop calling here. Please, stop calling." After a few weeks, Michael changed to an unlisted number, and the phone calls ended.

For a long time after, everything seemed okay, and Theresa even landed herself a decent job with the Detroit Institute of Arts. She couldn't quite afford to move out, but she told her parents that she would apply for an assistant director's job that would soon be open.

Coming down for coffee one morning, Catherine found Theresa crying at the kitchen table.

"What is it, honey? What's wrong?" Catherine asked. She sat and rubbed her hand across Theresa's shoulders.

"I'm scared," Theresa said, wiping the tears from her face.

"Why?"

"A few nights ago I got up to use the bathroom. I don't know why, but I looked out the window at the street. I saw Troy's car there." She sniffed and tried to compose herself.

"Are you sure?" Catherine pushed Theresa's hair away from her eyes.

"I know it was him. He was there last night, too." She stared into the table's centerpiece.

Catherine wasn't sure what to say.

"That's not all," Theresa said. "He comes to work all of the time, too. I always see him. He tries to talk to me— tells me that I have to give him another chance. I can't even walk through the place because I'm always worried he's there somewhere. He says he loves me even more than when we were together."

Catherine tried to think of a way to comfort her daughter.

"I think he's been in my office," Theresa continued. "In fact I know he has. When I came back from lunch the other day, a pair of earrings was sitting on my desk. There was a typed note underneath that said I should wear them with the red turtleneck I bought at the mall. How would he know where I bought that turtleneck?" Theresa set her face into her hands. "I think he's been going through my desk, too," she said after a few seconds.

Catherine imagined Troy going into the empty office. "Honey, don't worry. We'll tell your father."

Concerned by the story, Michael went to the police. They told him there wasn't really anything they could do because Troy hadn't done anything. They didn't pay too much attention to his request to have Theresa's desk finger printed. Determined to end the problem, Michael waited up a few nights to see if Troy's car would return. "Just to talk to the boy," Michael said. Catherine knew that's exactly what her husband would do. He was not a violent man, and she doubted whether he was even capable of violence.

When Troy's car arrived one night, Michael started down the driveway, but when the motion sensor set off the yard light, the car fired up and sped away. It never did return. When it hadn't returned for over a month, they assumed that the boy had moved on.

A few months later Theresa came home after a conference, burst through the door, and fell in front of where Catherine and Michael were sitting on the couch. They both rushed to her.

"What is it? What's wrong?" Even as they asked, Catherine felt it had something to do with Troy.

"He followed me," Theresa said in between short breaths. "He followed me from Kalamazoo all the way back home."

"Who?" Michael asked. "Troy?"

Theresa nodded. "That means he was there. He was in Kalamazoo the whole weekend. Just watching me. He knew where I was staying. He knew . . ." Her head dropped into her arms, and her sobbing shook her entire body.

"Are you sure it was him?" Catherine asked.

Theresa nodded wildly. "It was him. I know it was him."

"Well, that's it," Michael said. "The police are going to have to do something."

But, they didn't. They explained that there was nothing they could do until Troy actually did something. Driving behind someone on the highway, they said, was not a crime.

Michael didn't wait. Without any other options, he called Troy's father's business and waited while one secretary transferred him to the next. "Yes, I'll hold," Catherine heard him say a few times. Eventually he had Troy's father on the phone. Catherine listened while her husband cautiously explained what had been happening. After he was done explaining, he listened for a short time. "She's positive," he said once. Then after another minute he thanked the man and hung up.

After the phone call, nothing else happened. Theresa was promoted to assistant director and moved out a few months later. She soon started seeing a new man whom she'd met while out at a bar with a friend. Catherine didn't know too much about her daughter's new interest except what she could pick up from short telephone calls. What she knew for sure was that Theresa really enjoyed being with him. She said he was completely different from Troy. Still, Catherine was not prepared when her daughter called after only three months of dating to say that she was engaged.

* * *

Catherine glanced across the room and saw Bobby moving towards her table. He walked as though he was not in a hurry, spun once to talk to someone who was going by, and then walked again. In the shadowy light he looked like a teenager dressed for prom, though he was twenty-eight. She imagined the letdown he would be for her daughter. *He's never going to start that business.*

"Hi," Bobby said. He pushed both of his hands deep into his pockets.

"Hello," Catherine returned.

"Theresa wanted me . . . well, I wanted . . . I wanted to know if you would like to dance." He shrugged as he spoke.

Catherine listened to the fast beat of some modern song. She couldn't make out the lyrics except for something to do with "the reflex". The DJ's light show made it look as though all of the dancers were being electrocuted. She looked at Bobby.

"No, not to this song. I mean to a slow song." He pulled his left hand from his pocket and pushed it quickly through his hair.

Catherine wondered what kind of father he would be. She had guessed at first that a pregnancy had sparked their fast engagement. "No, Mom," Theresa declared, "You just don't know him, yet. I really love him."

Catherine studied Bobby as though he were a cardboard cutout. She wondered why her daughter didn't have better judgment, better taste. The man just didn't seem to have any real substance to him.

"I'll come back when there's a different song," Bobby said and then started to turn.

"Bobby," Catherine said. *He deserves to know about Troy, at least for his own safety,* she thought. Troy outweighed him by nearly one hundred pounds. His last victim, Theresa's study partner, had had his jaw wired shut for five months. "Sit down for a minute, please," she said.

Bobby pulled out a chair and sat. He crossed the fingers of his left hand into his right and set both on the table.

"Try not to go outside," Catherine said after a few seconds. She picked up her wine glass, but then saw that it was empty.

"What? Why?" Bobby asked. His left eye twitched slightly.

Catherine was quiet for a moment. "I don't know if she's ever told you . . . ," she started. "I mean . . . well, do you know about Troy?"

"Yes," he said solemnly, nodding. He unlocked his fingers and set both palms flat on the table.

"Well, he's here. He's in the parking lot across the street." Catherine saw what she guessed was fear paling Bobby's face. He swallowed hard once, took a deep breath, and then exhaled slowly.

"I don't think he'll come in," Catherine said. "I think he knows that we could call the police then." She saw how he listened to her, searching her eyes with his. *He looks so afraid*, she thought.

After a short silence Bobby stood.

"Don't tell Theresa," Catherine said. "She doesn't need to know about this. I think Michael is going to figure something out."

Bobby nodded and then turned and walked away. Catherine watched how he moved, as though he were in a daze. He crossed over to the bar, spoke to the bartender, and then lit a cigarette. After a few seconds the bartender set a beer in front of him. Catherine shook her head. She felt sorry for him — sorry that Troy was so much bigger than him, sorry that he would never be more than a house painter, sorry that her daughter would eventually leave him. Taking his beer, Bobby moved away from the bar into a nearby darkness. Catherine could no longer make him out among the other moving bodies.

A few songs later, Michael came towards her. He was shaking his head and his lips moved as though he were talking to himself. When he reached the table, she could smell the cold on him and knew that he'd been outside. He looked at her for a moment.

"What, Michael?"

He dropped down into a chair. "I went over to talk to him again. I offered him five hundred dollars to just leave." He made a small sweeping gesture with his hands.

"What? I hope you didn't give him money. I hope . . ."

"Don't worry. He didn't take it. He . . . he just said he's waiting for them to come out. He wants to talk to Theresa." Michael shrugged.

"No," Catherine said quietly.

"That's what he said he's going to do. He said he thinks she's making a mistake." Michael ran his left hand over his face.

"What's he going to do then? What's he . . . Can't we call the police now? Can't you call his father again?" A slightly metallic taste oozed into her mouth. Something like a low current of electricity tingled in her back.

"The police won't do anything, and I don't have his father's number here," Michael exhaled breathily.

While she wondered what they could do, Catherine saw something pale moving in the darkness near the bar, and then realized it was Theresa in her wedding gown. In the faint luminescence her dress made her look nearly angelic. Following Theresa, Catherine's father shuffled out of the darkness behind his cane.

"Look," Michael said, pointing towards Catherine's father.

"I see," she said. "What's he think he's doing?" she then whispered.

Theresa led the old man towards the dance floor. As she had earlier in the church, Catherine noticed that her father wore a new suit. It was only now that it suddenly meant something to her. In the past she knew him to have only one suit, a suit he'd worn to every occasion that warranted one — her mother's funeral, Theresa's graduation, and even Catherine's wedding so many years ago. At her own wedding, she had not found the time to dance with the man. She'd been too busy meeting people on Michael's side of the family — people who lived in Farmington Hills or Rochester Hills or Bloomfield Hills. She remembered seeing him out of the corner of her eye lingering around the edges of the dance floor, but he'd never quite caught her. And, she certainly hadn't made it easy the way she'd fluttered from table to table. Seeing him here now in a new suit, his arm shaking slightly as he hung his cane over the back of a chair, she felt something in her eyes, as though tears were welling. She could see how old he'd become. He was supposed to have died years ago from emphysema, but a Christmas card arrived from him each December addressed to *Mike* and *Cathy*. Opening it always reminded her that she needed to try to see him more often.

Her father's face was more determined than she'd ever seen it. Holding Theresa's hand, he hobbled forward. With each step it looked as though he might trip or collapse, but he seemed ready to will himself into a waltz, even if it meant a miracle. When they were finally a few feet onto the dance floor, he set his hand behind Theresa's back and began to move her. Leaves caught gently in the hem of her dress as he turned her in slow circles. Under the somewhat brighter lighting, the tree limbs and branches suspended above them suggested a scene from *A Midsummer Night's Dream*.

Catherine knew that she should have tried to stay closer to her father. Even now she only lived twenty-five minutes from him, and still sometimes a full year would pass before she would telephone to see if he was okay. And most times it was Michael who actually made the call. Catherine had wanted so badly to get out of the life that her father was able to provide that when she finally did, she never looked back. Now he was old. She wondered when next she would see him in his new suit.

Other couples cleared off the floor. Theresa leaned down and listened to something her grandfather said. A laugh burst from her and she cuffed him on the shoulder. Catherine remembered now that her father could always make people laugh. She recalled the men from the neighborhood gathered in their garage. While they worked on one neighbor's car or another, they listened to her father's stories about foremen at the factory. Their laughs had come forcefully, like birds trying to get out of them. She guessed that he had many qualities she hadn't really bothered to discover. To keep her tears back, she looked around the room and witnessed all the people who had stopped to watch Theresa and her grandfather dancing. She didn't see Bobby anywhere. *Of course this wouldn't mean anything to him*, she thought.

"Maybe we could sneak her out the back," Michael said, turning towards the table again. "I mean, have them both go out the back."

His words pulled her out of the moment and reminded her that Troy was still outside, waiting. She wished she could sneak Theresa out the back altogether. Sneak her right back to the moment that she'd met Bobby and then somehow intercede so the meeting would have never taken place. Or better, sneak her back to the moment she'd met Troy. She thought about all the other men her daughter could have met in college if she hadn't wasted those years with him.

"I just don't want her anywhere near him," Michael said, pointing his finger across the table towards nobody. He turned back towards the dance floor.

Catherine considered Michael's idea and guessed that it was for the best. They couldn't let Theresa know that Troy was outside or anywhere nearby. They certainly couldn't give him the chance to say something to her or to do something—not tonight of all nights. She leaned uneasily into her chair and watched her daughter and father dancing.

After a moment, she was aware of movement near the entrance of the hall. Looking past everyone who was turned towards the dance floor, she saw the groomsmen jostling into the room. One brushed his left sleeve with his right hand, and a thin cloud of dust rose off of it. Another's knees were brown with thick patches of ground-in dirt. One wiped the back of his hand across his face and called

Catherine's attention to the shiny blood in his mustache. The sleeve of his tuxedo was torn at the shoulder. *What have they been doing?* she thought. As she looked them over, she could see that they were all filthy, as though they'd left the reception to have a wrestling match. She could see too that their faces glowed with sweat. Despite their appearances, they were smiling, almost celebratory. Bobby walked in the middle of them. He wasn't dirty like the others, but every few seconds he shook his right hand and made a pained face. His groomsmen patted him on the back, and when they did he smiled broadly. After a short time, Catherine guessed where they'd been and what they'd done. Looking at the groomsmen, she guessed that it probably did take all of them to hold Troy.

They stopped under an auxiliary light just above the entrance. They craned their necks to see Theresa with her grandfather. Haloed by the light, the young men looked vibrant to Catherine—capable of nearly anything. She pictured the way they'd held Troy, the way Bobby's fist had landed in his stomach, against his cheek, on his nose. She took pleasure in thinking of Troy this way, and her feelings struck her as strange. Once she had hoped Troy would be her son-in-law. Looking at him, she saw Bobby cradle his hand while he watched the dancing. He held it close like an infant, and she hoped it would be all right.

Before First Light

Jeff Vande Zande

Watching Janet, his wife of five years, Hitch Olson guesses that she isn't in love with him anymore. Sometimes he isn't sure if he is in love with her. Other times, when things are good, he is sure. That's what makes it hard; he calls theirs a hard marriage. He is sure that there are people who have easy marriages. Though he hates the phrase, he is sure that there *are* soul mates. Hitch can't remember exactly when, but he knows at one time things were good between Janet and him. Then things seemed to get different, and he didn't think that they were as happy as they should be.

Janet sighs as she moves some plates from the dishwasher to the cupboard. The smell of salmon hovers in the room. Outside, headlights pull into a driveway and then go black, and Hitch wonders if his neighbor's marriage is happy.

"What's wrong?" he asks Janet. He's waiting for some kind of answer from her that will account for all of her sighing lately.

"Nothing," she says. She looks at him, smiles, and then goes back to the dishes.

Hitch doesn't believe her. Something in her smile is sad. He is sure she is hiding something. He is sure that in some way she is building up to telling him that she wants out. Watching her, Hitch feels their small kitchen constricting them, forcing them to the point of eruption.

"You're just sighing all the time," he says.

"I don't sigh all the time. I'm just tired." She pulls out the top rack and starts putting the glasses away. "The kids were really wild today. Thanksgiving break coming up and all."

Tired. Hitch knows what that means. He shakes his head. They hadn't had sex in three weeks. He takes a drink of his coffee; he likes to stay up at night and watch black and white movies. Since he was a kid he hasn't needed much sleep. "Why don't you have some coffee?" he says. He likes the way her dark hair falls into her face when she turns towards him.

"Not at six thirty." She looks at him for a second. Smiles. "Don't worry, Hitch." She closes the dishwasher.

"What?" He can feel his face reddening. He doesn't like where this is going. He feels he's been accused.

"I know you," she says. She grins at him and shakes her head.

"What?" he demands. He thinks she always makes him out to be some kind of sex-starved teenager. Sometimes he just wishes that she wanted him as much as he wanted her. Sometimes he just wishes that things were easy.

"I just know what you're worried about," she says. "But don't worry, we will."

"I wasn't thinking anything," he lies. "I just said because you're tired you should have some coffee, for chrissakes!"

The smile leaves her face. "Alright, you weren't thinking anything," she sighs. She turns her back to him and starts water for the pots and pans.

Hitch looks outside and sees that it's nearly dark. When he looks back towards Janet he thinks he sees her shaking her head. He wants to come up behind her and kiss her neck. He wants to make things right, but he's not sure he can. He looks out the window again.

He remembers that they used to talk more. When she'd get home from work, he'd talk to her about teaching. At one time he'd wanted to be a teacher. He liked when she talked about the kids who improved at reading or who suddenly figured out multiplication. It made his job as a systems administrator seem meaningless. For a while he thought about going back to school to become a teacher. Janet encouraged him. The University of Michigan had a campus in Flint, but Hitch decided that there was too much paperwork, too many meetings with counselors and advisors, too much work. Eventually, he stopped talking to Janet about teaching.

Why does this have to be so hard? he thinks. *This should be easier.* He knows that frustration with his marriage has been making him think about the past more. Lately it's been making him do some exploring on the Internet. A month ago he e-mailed Cindy Haywick, an old girlfriend of his. When he'd found her e-mail address on a special search website, something hot had risen to the surface of his skin and left his cheeks feeling sultry. Typing her a brief message, he had felt his heart thumping wildly in his chest. He hadn't felt anything like it in a long time.

After the first e-mail, Cindy started writing to Hitch almost every day. In response he didn't tell her much, only that he thought about her from time to time. He wondered if she was the girl he was supposed to marry. He remembers good things about being with her. They had talked all the time — in his car, at the movies, on the phone. He can't remember what they talked about, but it seems important to him that they had talked. Hitch recalls that he said a lot, and Cindy listened and laughed at things that he intended to be funny. He wishes it were like that with Janet. *And this isn't about sex*, Hitch thinks. *Christ, Cindy and I never even had sex. Anyone can have sex.*

Janet pulls the plug from the sink. Hitch listens to the water being sucked down. He watches Janet walk around the kitchen and wipe off the counter tops with a dishrag. "Jeopardy's on," she says, smiling. Hitch always watches Jeopardy with her. Sometimes, though, it bothers him that one of the only things they do together is watch television. "I'll be right in," he says. He watches her leave. Then he starts thinking about Cindy again.

They had dated for about seven months at the end of their senior year of high school. Both had applied to the same university, but Cindy didn't get in. Hitch had wanted to stay in town and go to the local community college with her, but neither she nor his parents would hear of it. Instead, Hitch and Cindy had said that they would give a long-distance relationship a chance. For a while Hitch talked to Cindy on the phone nearly every night. Then, as he met more people, he called her less and sometimes put off returning her messages. When she asked why, he told her that classes were getting busy. He didn't tell her about the parties. *I was so young, stupid,* Hitch thinks. Near the end of October of that first semester, he'd woken next to some girl in her dorm room, hung over and remorseful. He'd called Cindy that night. They talked for a long time. He didn't tell her what had happened, but they'd both agreed that a long-distance relationship was too hard. He wasn't sure if she too was meeting other people, but she'd agreed that they should break off from each other. Ten years later, it seems to Hitch that maybe he and Cindy had made a mistake. *If not, why do I keep thinking of her?* he thinks.

Hitch can hear Janet answering some of the questions from the show. Instead of joining her, he goes down to the basement to put his hunting gear together. Behind the closing door he thinks he hears Janet call his name, but he keeps going down. He twists the overhead bulb and uses its dim light to find his cedar trunk. The furnace clicks on and fills the silence with its drone. Handling his gear — his boots, his gloves, his blaze orange hat — makes Hitch feel good. Some of his favorite memories are of hunting trips with the guys. *Nothing ever changes up there,* he thinks, *it's always good times.* He stuffs his duffle bag and sees the box in the corner where he keeps his *Playboy* magazines. He hopes Janet never finds that box. *That would be a fight,* he thinks. Sometimes he regrets it, but at some point in their marriage Hitch had started lying to his wife to avoid hassles, disappointments, and inconveniences. *White lies*, he thinks. He throws a camouflage shirt over the box.

The box reminds him of the one time he'd seen Cindy nearly naked. She'd invited him to a family reunion at her uncle's cabin on Lake Huron. While the others were gathered around a bonfire on the beach, he and Cindy had snuck away to go night swimming. In the dark water, they'd found each other with lips and limbs. They'd gone farther than they'd ever gone before. He'd even thought they might make love, but then some of her cousins had come down to the water. They'd both thrashed about trying to find the top to Cindy's bikini.

In the cold basement, Hitch can still remember the way her body felt. He feels the heat in his own face. But above him Janet walks past. He feels guilty. *Christ, I haven't even done anything.*

In the morning he will be driving out of Flint to meet a few friends up north for the second weekend of deer season. Tomorrow evening he will meet Cindy at a bar just outside of Traverse City—at least that's what they'd worked out in e-mail. Cindy had written over and over again that she wanted to see him. *This isn't an affair,* he told himself. *I'm not even thinking of that.* He tries to remember what they used to talk about.

Coming upstairs over an hour later, Hitch finds the living room empty. He can hear the muffled dialogue of their bedroom television coming through the ceiling. *She wasted no time running up to bed*, he thinks. Turning the living room television on, he finds he's only missed the first fifteen minutes of *It's a Wonderful Life.*

Hitch watches the way Mary loves George Bailey. *Soul mates*, he thinks and shakes his head. He knows it's just a movie, but he can't help but think that some marriages are close to the Bailey's. He watches how Mary and George still love each other, even with all those kids. Janet talks about kids from time to time, even as recently as last week. *How the hell can she think about kids when we're falling apart?* he wonders.

Hours later, Hitch slips into bed and slips his hand up the back of Janet's pajamas. He begins to rub the muscles around her spine. He can smell her hair, like something earthy, on the pillows.

"Your hands are cold," she says.

"They'll warm up," he says. *She has to complain,* he thinks. But, he is glad that her voice makes her sound nearly awake. "The house is pretty cold."

She doesn't say anything, but she doesn't tell him to stop. After some massaging, he tries to make his rubbing more sensual, more insistent.

"I'm really tired," she says, as though he had asked a question. "It's so late, now. The principal wants to talk to all of us before school starts tomorrow."

In the past when he had rubbed like that she would turn in to him, push her lips into his. He doesn't know how to arouse her anymore. He pulls his hand out from under her top.

He stares up into the darkness. *In the kitchen she promised,* he thinks. *Now that we're in bed she renigs.* Her back towards him, he guesses that she is already sleeping. Then she stirs.

"It could be just for you, tonight."

Her wakeful voice in the darkness surprises him. "What?"

"I don't mind," she says. "I like to for you."

"That's okay," he says after a moment, even though he wants her to. He is still angry that it couldn't be for both of them. He wants to be like other married couples.

Nearly a minute passes. Hitch can hear the traffic halting and revving up to the rhythm of the neighborhood's stop signs.

"I really don't mind," Janet says again. She turns towards him and touches his chest.

"No, that's okay. Forget it," he says. He immediately wishes he would have said something different.

"Alright," she sighs and turns back on her side.

"What's wrong, now?" Hitch asks. He feels her pull the blankets around her tighter before she answers.

"Nothing is wrong, Hitch," she says. She stresses each word.

"It sounds like something is wrong," he says. He waits for her to say something, to say that she doesn't love him, to explain why things have been so different for the past couple years.

"Does something have to be wrong? What do I have to do? Should I smile all the time? Should I skip from room to room? What? Jesus, what do you want me to do, Hitch?"

"Nothing," he says. *Christ, it's like she hates me*, he thinks.

He lies in the darkness for a long time. *It's coming to an end. It has to be.* He thinks of Cindy and what he will say to her. He tries to remember what they used to talk about, but can't. Then, after some time, he is at the ocean, which fades into the bedroom again. Then he is wading out and an old friend is yelling to him from the beach about the undertow. The water is green and dark, but inviting. When he finds himself in his bed again, he is glad because he knows this preliminary dreaming means he will soon be asleep.

"What's it like in your blind in the morning?" Janet asks.

Hitch wakens fully. "What?"

"I just wanted to know what the woods were like that early in the morning," she says, turning towards him.

But she can't have sex, Hitch thinks. "It's cold. Christ, Janet, I was almost asleep. I thought it was so *late*."

"I'm sorry," Janet says. She doesn't say anything else.

Hitch tries to sleep again, but can't. The ocean does not return, and his mind stays locked awake. After some time he hears Janet's steady breathing. Her funny question stays with him. He thinks of waking her to tell her what it's like to be in the woods before dawn. Maybe then he could take her up on her earlier offer. *It's all too complicated*, he decides. When they'd first started going out she told him to wake her whenever he wanted to make love. He is pretty sure that offer is null and void. Frustrated, he eventually falls asleep.

* * *

Hitch begins to sober as he lies in Cindy Haywick's bed in her small apartment in Traverse City. She tells him that tonight is just what she needed. "Besides," she says, "I was always curious."

Waiting for her in the bar, he'd had four beers. He recognized her immediately when she arrived in her tight jeans and t-shirt. He'd offered her his hand, but she'd nearly jumped into his arms and then kissed him on the mouth. He had three more beers while she talked. She told him that she moved up north about four years ago with a boyfriend who wanted to start a charter boat fishing business. When the plans fell through, the boyfriend left and she stayed. For the past three years she lived with a guy who played guitar and sang for the tourists in the local bars. "That got old hearing the same songs every night," she'd said. "Plus, I think he slept around." Now she was working at a bank as a teller and trying to finish up her degree in radiology. Sometimes as she talked Hitch caught himself not listening.

"I haven't met a lot of friends up here," she'd said, placing one hand on his. Her other hand held a cigarette. Though Hitch tried, he couldn't say much to her because everything he knew was about his marriage. So, he listened to her, and drank, and when she invited him to her place for a nightcap, he went.

She lies with her hand on his chest. Then her hand starts to move down.

"I don't think again," he says. "I'm tired. I was up early." He wants to get out of the bed. He wishes he'd never climbed into it. He doesn't want to sleep in it.

"I'm tired, too." she says. "Will you be up here for long?"

"A few days." Hitch could smell her smoky breath. He could still feel everything about her, as though he were still having sex with her. *What the hell am I doing here?* he thinks. *How the hell did I let this happen?* He feels how empty his left hand feels without his wedding ring. He worries that it may have fallen from his pants pocket. He looks around the room, but it is too dark to see anything. What he can feel is the heat cranking out of the radiators. He feels constricted and kicks the covers off of himself.

I wanted to talk to her, he thinks. But he only knows how to talk about bills, bosses, house problems, and groceries. *Jesus,* he thinks, *what did we talk about before?*

"Have you ever been in the woods in the early morning?" he asks after a minute. It's the only thing he can think of.

Cindy doesn't say anything, but her hand moves on his chest.

"When you're walking out," he starts, "it's just like this. Black and silent. It's amazing how much noise your feet make. It's not warm like this, though. It's cold—a cold you can feel stiffen in your nose and burn your ears. And it's colder when you finally hunker down in your blind. You can really only see the trees at that time of the morning. And then they're just shadows. And the cold seems alive, the way it tries to get inside your clothes. That's when you question it. You wonder what the hell you're doing out in the woods at five in the morning. You wonder why you got out of a warm bed for all of this cold and dark."

He props himself up on an elbow and faces Cindy. He wishes he were getting up in the morning to hunt. He wishes he'd never sent Cindy that e-mail. Janet's face keeps trying to drift into his mind. He can feel himself trembling.

"But if you can keep from falling asleep and keep still enough to listen, you can hear the forest waking up. Everything begins to move. That moment of the morning is sometimes the best part of the hunting. Sometimes I feel like I'd like to live in that moment. Do you ever feel that way? Do you ever feel that you'd just like a moment to freeze so you can live the rest of your life in it?"

He waits for Cindy to answer. Then he can hear her steady breathing. She has fallen asleep. She hasn't heard anything he's said.

Below Zero

Jeff Vande Zande

Micky couldn't hear the neighbor's dog whining, and he thought that it might be dead. Earlier that evening, when he'd dragged the garbage cans down to the road, he'd felt the hairs in his nose stiffen. It was now easily well below zero. For the last two hours he had been in bed thinking and listening to the dog. Settling his head back into his pillow, he tried to remember if the animal had suddenly stopped or if it had faded into silence. In the day, constant barking boomed deeply from its throat, as though warning a stranger away. But for the past few nights Micky had been kept awake by the animal's sadder whimpering and yelping. He had never heard the dog at night before, but then Sheila had always slept with the television on. It had been nearly a week now since she'd left him. She was staying with a girlfriend until she figured something else out.

Micky cocked his ear towards the hallway. Listening, he heard nothing until the furnace whooshed on. Then silence again. Thinking of the dog freezing to death, he threw off his covers and shuffled down the cold hallway, but he couldn't see anything through the bathroom's frosted-over window. *Does the thing even have a little house to warm up in?* he wondered. Micky's own house knocked and pinged as it settled into its foundation. Walking on the balls of his feet towards the bedroom, he thought about how long *he'd* be able to stay. When she'd left, Sheila had said that she didn't even want the place. She'd said she wanted nothing that would remind her of their failed marriage. But, if she did file for a divorce, he guessed that she might become more interested in her share of their little cape cod. *Hell, even if she doesn't want the house, I can't afford it on my income alone,* he thought.

He crawled back onto his side of the bed. For the first few nights he'd tried to sleep in the middle, ready to start whatever this new life was going to be. Each morning, though, he woke on his side. *Of course, I'm just leaving room for her to come back any time she wants*, he thought. He missed the way she used to believe that there was something in him that could still surprise everyone. He missed her.

Micky strained to hear the dog again. Nothing. After a moment the toilet tank began to churn as it refilled itself. He'd meant to change the flapper for the past six months. In the darkness, the digital numbers of the alarm clock glowed back at him. **2:37**. He had to get up early to work a matinee, but he kept thinking about the dog. He wondered what it felt like to freeze to death. Was there pain until the end, but you just grew too weak to complain about it. Or was there no pain? Just a slight knowledge that something about this painlessness was numbing, even deadly.

When Micky was young his family had always had dogs, and he guessed that was why for as long as he could remember he'd told people that he was going to be a veterinarian. It's what he'd told Sheila when they'd started dating. It was only a few years ago that he'd convinced himself that loving dogs was a pretty childish reason to become a vet.

Micky pressed an ear into the cold mattress and pulled the cool side of the pillow over his other. It seemed silly to try to drown out silence, but at least this way he could tell himself that the dog had probably started barking again. He wondered what Sheila was trying to drown out all the nights that she'd slept in the noise of the television. Pulling the pillow off of his head, he propped it against the headboard and then lay into it, hands behind his neck. She'd said she was leaving because he never did anything. And, she could have lived with it had he seemed happy. But she'd said she couldn't live anymore with an unhappy man who was unwilling to do anything about his unhappiness.

Tonight while working his shift at the theater he'd had reason to remember everything he might have become. One of the other projectionists had left a textbook on the workbench in the projection booth.

Usually while Micky ran the late show he sat on his stool and watched a movie through the porthole. Sometimes he'd seen all the movies the theater was showing at least three times, but during the late show he always sat through another one. When a movie had a long run, he could sit on the stool and say the actors' lines a few seconds before they said them.

Tonight, though, he hadn't been able to keep his mind off of the textbook. His eyes wandered back again and again to the title along the book's spine: CHEMISTRY. He guessed that it would have been one of the courses he would have had to take to become a vet. Hefting the book, he studied the cover. A young man in a lab coat was using tongs to hold a beaker over a Bunsen burner. His wide eyes seemed to anticipate something marvelous. Behind him, blurred, a woman in a lab coat watched. Micky skated his fingers over the glossy cover. He paused over the blue flame as though he might feel some of its heat.

While the movies ticked through the projectors, Micky flipped through the pages. Eventually he turned to the first chapter and began skimming it. He was surprised that the words and formulas made sense to him; sciences had been among his better subjects in high school. After reading the first four pages, he flipped ahead to the problems for the chapter. He worked some of the problems on exponential numbers and scientific notation. As he figured the math, it was as though dry streambeds in his head had started to run again. He hadn't felt this way in a long time, and the only thing he could compare it to was the buzz he would get from a few beers. But still, it was a different kind of buzz.

The back of the book had the answers to the even problems, and Micky was surprised to see that he'd figured out numbers two, four, and six correctly. While still a senior in high school he had been accepted to a few colleges. He'd graduated twenty-sixth in a class of four hundred. But, like his friends, he'd decided to take a year off from school. Then he met Sheila. The year off became two years. When they learned that she was pregnant, they decided to marry. They'd always felt that they were going to get married anyway, and they took the accidental pregnancy as a good sign.

Soon after their small wedding, Micky started full-time as a projectionist in a downtown theater, which meant decent money. School wasn't on his mind at all. He could still remember coming back to their apartment, slipping into bed, and resting his palm on Sheila's swelling tummy. Even the doctor was surprised by the miscarriage.

There was nothing accidental about their next two years of trying to get pregnant again. Sheila eventually came out of the bathroom one morning pointing triumphantly at the blue line in the pregnancy test, but a month later a doctor was explaining to them why that one didn't take. And from there it seemed like everything started to miscarry. *We just gave up*, Micky thought. *Or at least I gave up*, he thought a moment later.

Micky rolled on his side, tried to sleep, but then thought about the dog again. *Maybe someone let him in*, he thought, but then he imagined his neighbor—a single guy who worked third shift at the nearby cannery. *That sonuvabitch doesn't deserve a dog's loyalty*, Micky thought. Closing his eyes, he could hear the way the neighbor yelled out the window for the dog to shut up. Of all the times he had seen the neighbor go into his house, he'd never seen him with anything other than fast food. The guy disgusted him, and Micky wondered if that's how Sheila felt when she thought of him. He remembered how disgusted she'd seemed a few weeks ago while she was hanging her Valentines decorations.

"I guess I can understand Christmas," Micky said. The television program he was watching had gone to commercial and he looked over at Sheila where she stood on the couch in front of the picture window. A red silhouette of a cupid blossomed from the fingers of her left hand. "I just don't get hanging Valentines decorations. Seems like a waste."

"It brightens up the place for a few days," Sheila said. Pressing a piece of tape over the fishing line, she pulled her hands away. The cupid swung back and forth in the center of the window. She bent down into the box again.

Micky hadn't done anything, but he felt exhausted. "Well, I'm not helping," he said, turning back towards his show.

"I didn't ask you," she said. She stood with a large heart dangling from her fingers.

"I know you think I should help, but I just want to sit here," he said.

"Jesus, Micky, so sit there."

"I just think what you're doing is a stupid waste of time." He turned up the television.

"Ah, Micky," Sheila sighed. She dropped the heart and walked out of the room.

As he lay in bed, he recalled that she hadn't said anything right away. She'd stood on the couch with the heart hanging from her fingers for moment. Thinking of her that way made him the most miserable he'd been since she'd left. He knew that he hadn't always been this way, but he couldn't remember how to be anyone other than the man he'd become. Finding the remote control, he turned on the television to keep himself from crying.

He tried to find something to watch, but mostly there were infomercials. Suspiciously enthusiastic men with ponytails yelled at him about their great new cleaning products or exercise equipment. Micky watched one man pour ketchup, mustard, chocolate syrup, grape jelly, and cranberry juice onto a white dress shirt, shouting out the name of each as he dumped it on. A canned audience moaned their repugnance as the shirt became more filthy.

"Now," the man bellowed, "I'll set the shirt in one gallon of water, add a teaspoon of Stain Away, and then stir." He picked up what looked to Micky like a chopstick and began spinning the shirt through a punchbowl of water. After a few seconds, he stopped stirring and the camera followed him over to another punchbowl. Reaching in he pulled out a clean shirt that looked exactly like the other. "If I would have kept stirring that other shirt for three minutes, this is what it would have looked like. But I don't have three minutes. I need every second I can get to tell you more about the cleaning product that's literally going to change your life!"

Micky turned the television off. *I wish I could change my life*, he thought. *I wish someone would pick me up, drop me in some water, and stir me clean.* Recalling the many stains of his life, he wondered why Sheila hadn't left him sooner. *Christ, how many times did I promise her I was going to start classes?* he wondered. Semester after semester he'd vowed to take at least one course, but he always found some reason why he couldn't get around to registering. Registering would have been easy enough, but it always struck him that it would just take too long to graduate if he only took two classes a year. Instead, he had wanted to wait until they came into some money or saved enough that he could go to school full time. Rolling onto his back and staring up into the darkness, he realized what a naïve plan he'd had. He figured out that if he had started taking one class each semester, including spring and summer, he would now have a couple dozen courses finished. He wondered if Sheila had done the same math.

He rubbed his eyelids. Outside he heard a car slow for the stop sign on the corner. A few seconds passed, but he didn't hear it accelerate again. Rolling onto Sheila's side of the bed he looked out the window and could see the car's brake lights. It idled for what seemed like a long time, and then finally the driver edged into the intersection and crawled from Micky's view. *Probably drunk* Micky thought.

It made him wish that he had beer in the fridge, something to help him sleep, but he hadn't shopped since Sheila had left.

What the hell was I thinking? Micky thought. *I blew every chance I had.* Two years ago Paul Olson had retired as the manager of the theater. Micky had mentioned it in passing to Sheila, and she had started encouraging him to apply for the job. "You've been there longer than anyone," she'd said. "Why don't you apply? You'd be good." For the next few days she'd kept after him about the position.

At the time Micky hadn't seen the job for what it could be. He'd felt it would have left him trapped, locked into a career that probably wasn't right for him. He guessed that if he took the job that he would never go to college.

"Jesus Christ, Sheila," he'd started when she'd asked for the fifth time if he was going to apply. "Do you really think they're going to hire me? I'm twenty-six. Olson was in his seventies. Probably started when he was in his forties. They're not looking for a god damn kid. And besides, what the hell do I know about managing anything?"

He never did apply, and three weeks later he found a memo in his box announcing that Jeremy Fisher, a twenty-three year old junior in college that Micky had trained in on the projectors, was going to be the theater's new manager. A job like that would have meant ten thousand more a year for them, not to mention benefits. As it was now, he got his medical insurance from the dentist office where Sheila worked as a receptionist.

Micky winced and tried to push the memory of his blunder from his mind. *I'd do it differently now*, he thought. *If I'd known what she was really thinking, I'd have done the whole thing differently.* In all the years that he'd been married to her, he had never once imagined Sheila leaving him.

He got up out of bed again and shuffled back to the bathroom. The window was still frosted over, and he rubbed his hand across it. He half expected to be able to rub a hole through, but then realized that the frost was on the other side. Bending closer, he saw that the icy veneer was actually made up of what looked like hundreds of snow flakes flattened frozen against the glass. It made him think of the way something that seemed insignificant like the passing of days could eventually pile up into an icy sheet of years.

Micky knocked his fist against the glass. Then he listened. *Why the hell doesn't the thing bark?*

He stepped back from the window and sat down on the lid of the toilet. He set his face into his hands.

"God damn it" he said, feeling his tears against his palms. *How the hell do you change things? How the hell do you go in a different direction?*

He wondered what kind of movie his life would make. *Who the hell would go?* he thought. But he knew Sheila had bought a ticket and had waited seven years for something to happen in the plot. *She waited as long as she could stand it,* he thought. He pictured her sitting in a theater watching a scene of him on the couch. Then he saw himself in the projection booth loading another reel of depressing footage onto a projector. *If it were anything like that,* he thought, *I'd just splice a different ending on for her – scenes from a happier movie.*

The toilet tank hished again as it filled with water. Almost immediately Micky felt that he would burst if he didn't do something. He flipped on the light and pulled the lid from the tank. Even as he reached down into the cold water he knew there was nothing he could do without a new flapper. He pulled his dripping hands out and put the lid back.

I've gotta do something, he thought. He wondered what Sheila would think if he called her. *I could tell her what I've been thinking.* But he knew, even as he thought it, that Sheila wasn't interested anymore in his thoughts. He'd been thinking about doing things for too long. He knew she needed more than thinking from him.

Starting back toward the bedroom he paused and listened for the dog one last time. *That poor sonuvabitch might still be out there*, he thought. It then struck him what he had to do.

Going down barefoot, he could feel where the top few steps of the stairs that he'd refinished gave way to the rougher steps that he'd never gotten to. On some steps he could feel stray staples from where they'd pulled up the carpet when they'd first moved in.

Feeling his way to the foyer, he pictured his boots in the kitchen where he'd kicked them off earlier. *The hell with them*, he thought. *I'm not going to be out there long.* He opened the front door, ran down the icy porch steps, and sprinted to the neighbor's wooden privacy fence. While he was running, he'd felt the cold stinging his feet, but when he stopped the feeling changed, as though the cold had started sinking teeth into him. A feeling shot up from his soles, traveled along his inner thigh, and settled in his crotch — giving him a sudden urge to urinate. *I don't think I can stay out here*, he thought, hopping from foot to foot. Though the bottoms of his feet seemed resistant, the tops burned frigidly under the snow.

I can't stop now, he decided. His heart felt like something alive trapped in his chest. Reaching over the top of the door he flipped the latch, but when he yanked the handle, a twinge burned in his shoulder. The door barely budged. Its base had at least a foot and a half of snow packed against it.

His feet started to numb, but he pulled at the door again with both hands. If the dog was alive he was going to take it home, keep it. *Dogs deserve better than this*, he thought. After more pulling he'd made a slight opening. He pressed his body into it and squeezed into the backyard. The space was bigger than he thought it would be. For a moment he stood in the cold blackness, unsure what to do next. Then he whistled and clapped his hands.

Jeff Vande Zande

Cinnamon Ant

Jeff Vande Zande

My father wades waist-deep in the bend upstream, and from this distance he doesn't look anything like a woman. Even though he and his fly rod are in silhouette, I recognize his technique. His back cast always went up too high. He's never been graceful with a rod, and I can see that estrogen hasn't done much to help that. Estrogen. Jesus Christ.

Casting to the left bank, he startles a heron into flight. Its big wings lift it slowly out of the shallow water where it's been hunting for minnows or frogs. At first its takeoff is labored, almost lumbering, as though it were never meant for flight. It looks as though it's drowning in the air. It's an ugly bird—the prehistoric S of its neck, the spindly legs coming out of the body as if Abby, my daughter, had drawn them. I guess, though, that she's probably better at drawing now.

Soon, with a slight adjustment of its wings, the heron begins to fly across the river and then out of sight over the yellowing trees. Something about the shift straightens out its appearance. It becomes handsome, almost beautiful. My father turns his head to watch it, and I see that he has grown his hair long and wears it in a bushy ponytail. Christ, this is going to be hard. It's been so long since I've seen him. Her, I mean. Her.

Two times on the way here I had my car in a driveway, ready to turn around, but both times I ended up back on the road towards the river. I don't know, maybe I just couldn't take another Saturday of watching television and pacing the three rooms of my nearly unfurnished apartment. I didn't think I'd be so bad at being alone.

It was Dad's idea to meet this way. He explained that he'd park about a half mile upstream from our old spot and fish his way down. I was thankful because I don't think I could have driven here with him. Too much too fast. He claims he wanted it this way so he could work the rust out of his casting arm. I don't know if I believe him. I have the sense he was sparing me the shock of pulling up next to his vehicle and having him get out. Bam! Here's your dad, except now he's a woman. I like this way better. He can work his way to me gradually, and I can try to get used to her.

He's fishing differently than I've ever seen, working the bank closely as he always used to, but once in a while flicking a cast to the middle of the stream. In the past he'd always said that a fly, at least in the day, has no business in the middle. "Only fingerlings and creek chubs feed in the middle," he would say. "The big boys are in the shadows." He's not as focused as he used to be. Sometimes he stops and studies something along the banks—sometimes long enough that his line goes taut. He'd never done that in the past. "My fly's either in the air or moving with the current," he always used to say, especially when he was explaining to me why he'd caught so many more fish than I had on a given day.

Watching him, I start to feel drugged, unable to move or think. It's a way I get sometimes lately—thinking so hard that my mind falls into a numbed thoughtlessness. I think about Susan and Abby all the time, but I don't know why I bother. Nothing's going to change.

I snap myself out of it. As I make my way to the bank, the river pushes against me. It feels good to be working against a current again. It feels good just to be doing something. Once into the shallow water, I rest the butt end of my rod in some branches near shore. It's a trick Dad taught me to free up my hands. The only things he ever did teach me had something to do with fishing.

Running my line through the guides, I lose myself in the motions of getting ready. The leader I have on is still about six feet long. Good. I don't think I could handle a nail knot. Not now. I open my day box. It's late in the season, so just about anything will draw trout. I choose an elk-hair caddis. It takes me a few attempts to thread my tippet through the hook, and it takes me several more tries to remember the knot I'm supposed to use. It's a special knot that doesn't cut against itself under pressure. My father called it a fisherman's knot. I don't know, maybe he calls it a fisherperson's knot now.

The sky is almost all blue with only a few wisps of clouds in the eastern horizon. I had hoped for a little more overcast. Casting a short distance upstream, I see the hair-thin shadow coming from the tippet as my fly floats by. The trout will spook easily today. Still, my cast wasn't bad at all for five years away from the rod. I start casting at some likely spots — places where the water eddies in pockets before a log then where it runs along side the log and then in the scum line beyond the log. I'm edgy, waiting for the surface to rip open under my fly, but nothing happens. Too goddamn sunny. We're not going to catch any fish today. After several more casts it starts to really settle in on me that my father's coming down the river towards me.

He'd somehow heard that Susan had left me. The news had taken a while to get to him too because we'd already been separated for over a year. I didn't know who it was when I'd picked up, and I was surprised as hell when Dad told me. His voice was still gravelly, but slightly higher. It wasn't really womanly though. He told me that he'd heard what had happened to Susan and me. It's funny too because he'd never even met her. I didn't even try to invite him when she and I tied the knot.

During the phone call he said he wanted to take me fishing. Some things don't change. It was my father's way to take me fishing any time there was a problem. I remember the last time we fished together was after we'd learned that Mom wasn't going to get better.

We never talked about what was going on in our lives when we were on the river. For the few hours we were there the water was the only place we had to live. Our talk was of rises and hatches and new deadfalls. When we'd get off the water, the problems and the feelings were still there, but there was something good about the respite. It's what my father had to give me—a little breather. I suppose that's what he's trying to do now.

"What are you using?"

His voice is right behind me. Taking a breath, I turn to face him, but the way the sun reflects off the surface between us I can only see an outline of him.

"Caddis," I say. I start to reel my line in.

"I think they want terrestrials today," he says. "I'm using a cinnamon ant. I've already had four fish. I released a ten-inch brookie around the bend back there."

The sun still blinds me from seeing him. I'm not even sure I'm hearing him right. My father had always made a point of keeping his flies secret from me. Sometimes I'd go through an entire leader tying on new flies, and the whole time he'd be filling his creel. "It kinda floats," he'd say if I asked him for any details about his fly. When I was younger he'd almost get me crying. When I got older, I'd just quit fishing and go wait for him in the truck. Sometimes I waited until past midnight.

"Did you say you released a fish?" I remember he used to step on under-sized fish to press them out to legal.

He tells me he didn't bring a creel. Squinting into the glare, I hear the small click of his day box and a few seconds later the snap of its closing. "You want one of these cinnamon ants?" He steps forward into the shadows of a tree.

I'm not really aware of anything except his red hair. He always used to wear it very short—military style. I never even knew it was wavy until now. A purplish bandana holds it in a ponytail. Then I see his hand. It's my father's hand—bulky, freckled, knuckles the size of olives. The orange ant is pinched between his thumb and forefinger, but I mainly see his fingernails, grown out like a woman's and painted the same color as his bandana. I'm aware that I'm trying not to look into his face. Studying the ant, I see that whatever hormones he might be taking have done little to shrink his thick forearm or thin out the hair that sweeps down it.

"That's what they're biting on," Dad says, and I can tell he's saying it just to prompt me to do something other than stand in the water staring at his hand.

I take the ant, but it doesn't feel right. Holding it makes me feel a little sick inside, like he just handed me a nipple. I hook the ant to my fly patch. "I just tied on the caddis," I say.

He reaches out and pushes his fingers through my hair. "You're starting to thin out," he says.

I jerk my head back quickly, and he does the same with his hand. Though it feels like everything is frozen, the rivers still rushes past, pushing against our legs. I want to bolt for the car and get the hell out of here, but I can't move.

"You're still handsome, though," he says. "I mean, even with the thinning." Fortunately, after saying that, he moves towards the right bank and attempts a roll cast.

I can barely lift my arm to fish. Everything feels heavy. Of all things, why'd my dad have to become a woman? I mean, if he'd just have left after Mom died I could have lived with it. I feel like packing up and starting over myself sometimes. Hell, I feel like that a lot. I wouldn't have blamed him. But why did he have to send me that letter? Why did he have to let me know what he was doing to himself? Everything I think about lately is a question. Why does my job feel like something I've been sentenced to? Why did Susan and I fall apart? Why did I have to slap her that night? What did she mean when she said the slap might have been just what she needed? Why haven't I made an effort to see Abby?

What locks me up is I can't answer any of the questions.

My dad has worked his way ahead of me, and from behind, except for the hair, he looks like his old self. Out of character, though, he's spending way too much time on some unlikely water. Dead water. The river is wide here and spreads itself into a slow, shallow run, especially where he is fishing. In the past he'd have walked right through this stretch, but today he works it as though it's as promising as anything. He must see that I have the good side where the current riffles near the bank and provides some likely runs where trout might feed. Ahead of me the surface dimples with small rises, and a feeling runs warm and tingly through my blood that gets me casting again. I start to remember why I always liked fishing.

After several casts I can't get anything that's in the riffle to rise to my caddis. I can see the cinnamon ant on my vest patch, but I guess that it wouldn't make a damn bit of difference. Just not worth all the effort of retying. The small run I'm fishing eddies in front of a large, submerged boulder. I guess that bigger fish might be settled in there waiting for the current to bring food down into the slower swirl. I edge my way closer to cast to the pool, trying not to kick up any silt. When I get in casting distance, a fingerling bursts out of the water after a dragonfly that's flying low over the surface. The insect is nearly as big as the trout. It dodges the attempt and flies away. After a few seconds, the small fish launches itself above the surface again, and I breathe a small laugh through my nose and shake my head. It's comical really. Little fish all hopped up on life acting like anything is possible. It gets me thinking about Abby.

She was as wild as anything. Sometimes her energy and smile could even jolt me enough that I'd drag myself off the couch, shut off the television, and play dolls for a while. Dolls, tea party, drawing . . . whatever she wanted to play. But that wasn't very often. Most of the time I'd stay on the couch and flip through channels and just try not to think about everything I had to do. The house. The bills. My job.

Abby would jump around, spring from the lazyboy to the couch, run from the kitchen to the living room. A lot of times I just sat there waiting for her bedtime. I was so tired. "Did she get a nap today?" I'd ask Susan, hoping she'd say no. No nap meant earlier bedtime.

"Why don't you just play with her? Wear her out a little," Susan would say.

"Jesus Christ, I just got home from work. Can't I just sit down for a minute?" But I seldom sat down for only a minute. Usually I'd sit there for three hours with Abby springing around in front of me like that fingerling trout. She was so full of life she couldn't contain it. And there I sat so weighed down with everything I'd let get under my skin. If it were now, right now, I'd be on that floor with her. Nothing would stop me from playing with her. But I don't really know if I'm going to get the chance to play with her again. Not after that night.

"Do you ever say yes?" Susan asked me. "And the look you get on your face . . . like you want to spit on me. For six months now that's the look you've given me. I wish I had a mirror sometimes."

She'd just asked me if I wanted to go blueberry picking the next morning. She was right, too. I hadn't heard much of what she'd said. "Tomorrow morning we could get up, drive to . . ." she'd started, but by then I was already shaking my head.

"What do you want to do then?"

I shrugged.

"You see. What am I supposed to do with that? You don't *want* to do anything. I can't take it anymore. You don't even help out with Abby . . . you don't even play with her."

We'd already put Abby to bed for the night. I worried that Susan's raised voice was going to wake her.

"I do too. Sometimes."

"What do you do, Chuck? Tell me what you do. Do you feed her? Do you bathe her? Do you ever get up at night with her?" She was getting louder.

"I'm at . . ."

"I know. I know. You're at *work* all day. And you're *tired* when you come home."

"Yeah, that's right, I am tired. If you had any idea . . ."

"I wish that was it. I could take you tired." She drowned me out. "But you're not just tired. You're dead. You drag yourself around here like a zombie. I just can't stand it anymore. I can't, Chuck. You're killing us. I want to know when things are going to be different! Damn it, I want to know! Tell me! Just tell . . ."

She was screaming by then, looking right up into my face. I'd never seen her get like that. My hand came out of nowhere. It's like when you're walking down the river and suddenly you walk right into a deep hole before you can stop yourself. In seconds your waders are full of water and you're miserable.

She threw me out that night, and I left without a word. Grabbing some clothes, I tried not to look at her. I couldn't take seeing that one cheek redder than the other. I did whatever she said. I mean, I'm not a wife beater. I really hated myself, even though she kept telling me that she wasn't throwing me out because of the slap.

"Charlie! Big one on," my dad yells over his shoulder. With his excitement, his voice is much higher, much more feminine. It reminds me of the way Susan's voice used to get when we were first dating and I'd take her bluegill fishing.

It looks like the fish hit Dad's fly near the far end of the dead water. His line slices through the surface as the fish swims hard toward a windfall near the far bank. If it gets into the submerged branches it has a good chance of tangling the line and wrenching the hook from its mouth. When the fish is nearly into the fallen tree, Dad takes a step back and then a step downstream. I wait for the line to go loose and come sailing out of the water, but it doesn't. It stays taut, and the tree is no longer in the fish's reach. Changing strategies, it takes off downstream.

"I haven't got a net!" my dad screams. Letting up slightly with his left hand, he gives the fish some line so it can swim farther and tire itself out.

I pull my net from my back and shout that I'm coming behind him. He starts to retrieve the line and pull the fish in. I can see he doesn't want it to get into a mild run of rapids about fifty yards downstream. Swimming in the rocky bottom it could rub the hook out of its mouth.

For nearly ten minutes Dad keeps the fish in a stretch that offers little in the way of escape. The bottom is sandy, the water near the banks is shallow, and there are no logs.

I stand next to him ready with the net. We don't say anything to each other, but I can hear Dad whispering to the fish. "Go ahead," he says, "Get it out of your system. Yeah, there you go. You're feeling tired now, aren't you?"

The line zigzags slowly as the fish looks for someplace safe. Sometimes it circles back to where it's just been. It's beyond desperate now – just dazed and fatigued. I guess I know what it's feeling. Even now, waiting for Dad to land what might be the biggest trout I've ever seen, I can't stop thinking about Susan and Abby. "The slap is nothing," Susan said the last time I tried to apologize again. "It's you. You're not who I married." That's what leaves me feeling trapped. I don't remember how I used to be. And that's what's hard. I want to be that way again.

"You see it! Jesus, it's big," my dad says.

The fish is about fifteen feet from us. It comes up close to the surface and shows the mossy yellow of its belly. It's a big brown—well over twenty inches.

"Get the net ready." Dad starts to pull his line in, and I can see the dark shadow swaying and rocking closer to us. It looks as though it's giving up, almost swimming willingly above the submerged net.

When I lift up the fish folds. Hitting the air, it flips a few more times against the mesh, but I can see that it has almost nothing left. I should be excited, but I feel tired too.

My dad puts a few fingers into the brown's gills and lifts it from the net. Before I can tell him that it probably won't fit in my creel, he walks it out to the middle of the stream. I follow him.

"Good fighter," he says, setting the brown back in the water. When he releases his grip the fish, looking dead, begins to roll downstream. Dad catches it and holds it steady in the current.

"You're not going to keep it?" I ask.

"No. Do you want it?"

I look at the fish. It's starting to move slightly from side to side. Or maybe it's just the wavering effect of the water. "No, I don't want it."

Dad's still crouched over the fish. He holds it this way for a while. I watch his hands.

I guess he's trying to oxygenate him, trying to revive him. I've read about it in some fly fishing magazines — the ones that promote catch and release. I've also read that he's dead no matter what Dad does. Some say getting caught just shocks the fish's system too much. Others say that touching the fish at all strips a protective mucous from it. I don't know. I guess I lean toward the idea that the fish is a goner.

"Here he goes," Dad says. The fish wrenches from his grip and shoots upstream like a small torpedo. "Feels like he's going to make it." He works his way over to the bank. In the past he would have had a smoke, but he doesn't light up. Hell, in the past he would have been cleaning that fish. I sit down next to him in the wet grass along the bank.

We don't say anything to each other. I watch the river for rises. Then I study the surface to see what insects are floating by. But, no matter what I try to think about, I keep coming back to Susan and Abby. I just can't lose myself in the fishing like I used to.

"I was really sorry to hear about you and Susan," my dad says, as though reading my thoughts.

I pick a stone out of the black mud and try to skip it, but it hits the water once and disappears.

"It must be hard on Abby," he says after a moment.

I want to tell him that it's hard on me too, but I just nod my head. I don't tell him that I haven't seen Abby in over six months, even though she's only across town.

"I want you to tell me something," he says. He picks up a stone. "Do you think Mom and me had anything to do . . . I mean, we weren't good for each other. The arguing. You heard a lot. Saw a lot of cold times. Do you think that . . . or do you think me, what I did, did that make it harder for you? I mean, to be with someone?"

I want to tell him that it felt pretty fucked up to have my widower dad skip town and become a woman, but that's not really what he asked. "I don't know. I guess I don't really buy into that," I say. "I guess Susan and I didn't need any help falling apart."

"Maybe," he says. He skips his stone and it hops across the surface and lands on the other bank. "Still, though, when I heard . . . it's just I know I wasn't much of a father . . . I mean even before."

"I don't really know why it happened," I say. I don't tell him about the slap. I also don't tell him that for the last two years I've felt that there's something I need to be doing – something I can't name. It eats at me, even though I can't picture it, and everything else in my life seems to be keeping me from it. Fifty hours a week at the hospital supervising data processors—doing what I can to monitor their accuracy. Every Thursday morning sitting in the conference room hearing about the mistakes my people made. Every time they key a digit it could come back to me. What kind of job is that? I guess it's the kind of job you can't walk away from once you've had a few raises.

And then Susan and her waiting for me at the door all the time with that look on her face, like she needed me to say something that would lift her up. She looked hungry. I didn't ever try to imagine what it was like to be with an infant all day. It must have eaten at her, but I never brought anything home but my own heaviness, my own darkness. Even for Abby I had nothing, just enough to keep from yelling at her about stupid things. I know exactly what Susan's talking about when she tells me I've changed. Sometimes I can step outside myself and hear my words and watch the way I drag myself around.

"Christ, Dad, I don't know. Susan tells me I'm not the same anymore. She says it's like I've partly died. And, I know what she means. But I don't know. It just seems so hard to do anything about it. What do you think . . . I mean, do you think people can ever change?"

For a few seconds he's silent, and then he bursts out laughing. I've never heard my father laugh this way. It's throaty and broken loose, like something wild he can't keep in.

I turn and really see his face for the first time that day. A jolt of something crawls up the center of my back, though I'm not exactly repulsed. Lipstick, rouge, eyelashes, eyeliner, earrings – none of it really covers my dad's thick chin, busted nose, and ruddy skin. He's one of the ugliest women that I've ever seen, but he's a woman. I see that now. He's a woman.

There's just something feminine about his face that goes deeper than the makeup. Maybe something is different about his eyes. I can't put my finger on it, but he's definitely no longer a man.

When Dad sees the way I'm studying her face, she starts to laugh into her hand. "I'm sorry," she says, still choking down laughter. "I'm not laughing at . . ."

"It's all right." I start laughing too. I can't help it.

Dad starts laughing hard again. "I go by Carol now," she gets out.

"It's a nice name," I chuckle. Laughing this way feels really good.

We take turns skipping stones for a while as our laughing idles down.

"I wish I could meet Abby sometime," my dad says.

Like that, the laughing is over. I try to say something, but I can't find any words that make sense. I feel like the wind was knocked out of me.

Dad skips a few more stones then gets up. "I'm going to work downstream, I think." She uses my shoulder to push herself up, and I let her.

I wonder if I could call Susan and arrange a visit. I haven't seen Abby in a long time. It's in my rights to see her. No lawyers have said otherwise, yet. "I'll fish behind you a hundred yards or so," I shout. Dad lifts her hand. I sit for a while and let her get ahead of me. She's working her way to a bend where the river sweeps hard to the west and out of sight. When she gets to the bend, I'll start behind her. As I remember, there's some good water around that bend – good cover, good riffles.

When she's nearly a football field from me I see her rod bend again. This fish isn't nearly as big as the last, but it looks decent. Watching Dad for a minute, I see that her body is different. Maybe it's the light, but I think I see an hourglass shape to her—even through the waders and the vest. It's slight, but it's there.

I wonder why Susan hasn't gone further with our separation. Why hasn't she filed for a divorce? Why hasn't she moved out of town? She always used to talk about living anywhere but Michigan. I need to call her. I need at least to arrange it so that Dad can meet Abby.

Dad will soon fade around the bend. Before I follow, I clip my caddis off and begin to tie on the cinnamon ant. I suck on the knot to moisten it before I tighten it. Dad taught me that it helps reduce the friction—helps keep the knot from breaking. If I get something big on later, I don't want to lose it.

Jeff Vande Zande

Jeff Vande Zande was born in Michigan's Upper Peninsula. "Its long winters helped me see that people are at their best when they are helping other people." It was also in the Upper Peninsula's spare job market that Vande Zande first started to look for work. Finding it, he quickly learned that the living a job can provide can also be a type of dying. Among other jobs, he's worked as a dishwasher, furniture mover, janitor, welder, projectionist, and maintenance man.

He now lives in Michigan's Lower Peninsula in Bay City with his wife, son, and daughter. In addition to other courses, he enjoys teaching developmental writing and reading at Delta College. In addition to fiction, Vande Zande also writes poetry. In 2002, Partisan Press released his *Last Name First, First Name Last*. March of 2003 saw the release of his chapbook of poems, *Tornado Warning* (March Street Press). Currently, he is at work on a novel that continues the story of Stan Carter from "Downstream Water" in this collection.

****** **Working Lives Series** ******
Bottom Dog Press
http://members.aol.com/lsmithdog/bottomdog
Robert Flanagan. *Loving Power: Stories*. 1990/ 0-933087-17-9 $8.95
A Red Shadow of Steel MIlls: Photos and Poems. 1991
(Includes Timothy Russell, David Adams, Kip Knott, Richard Hague)
0-933087-18-7 $8.95
Chris Llewellyn. *Steam Dummy & Fragments from the Fire: Poems*.
1993/ 0-933087-29-2 $8.95
Larry Smith. *Beyond Rust: Stories*. 1996 / 0-933087-39-X $9.95
Getting By: Stories of Working Lives. 1996
eds. David Shevin and Larry Smith / 0-933087-41-1 $10.95
Human Landscapes: Three Books of Poems. 1997
(Includes Daniel Smith, Edwina Pendarvis, Philip St. Clair)/
0-933087-42-X $10.95
Richard Hague. *Milltown Natural: Essays and Stories from a Life*. 1997
0-933087-44-6 $16.95 (cloth)
Maj Ragain. *Burley One Dark Sucker Fired*. 1998 / 0-933087-45-4 $9.95
Brooding the Heartlands: Poets of the Midwest, ed. M.L.Liebler. 1998
0-933087-50-0 $9.95
Writing Work: Writers on Working-Class Writing. 1999
eds. David Shevin, Larry Smith, Janet Zandy / 0-933087-52-7 $10.95
Jim Ray Daniels. *No Pets: Stories*. 1999/ 0-933087-54-3 $10.95
Jeanne Bryner. *Blind Horse: Poems*. 1999 / 0-933087-57-8 $9.95
Naton Leslie. *Moving to Find Work: Poems*. 2000 / 0-933087-61-6 $9.95
David Kherdian. *The Neighborhood Years*. 2000 / 0-933087-62-4 $9.95
Our Working Lives: Short Stories of People and Work. 2000
eds. Bonnie Jo Campbell and Larry Smith / 0-933087-63-2 $12.95
Allen Frost. *Ohio Trio: Fictions*. 2001/ 0-933087-68-3 $10.95
Maj Ragain. *Twist the Axe: A Horseplayer's Story* 2002/
0-933087-71-X $10.95
Michael Salinger. *Neon: Stories & Poems*. 2002 / 0-933087-72.1 $10.95
David Shevin. *Three Miles from Luckey: Poems*. 2002 /
0-933087-74-8 $10.95
*Working Hard for the Money: America's Working Poor in Stories,
Poems, and Photos*. 2002, eds. Mary E. Weems and Larry Smith /
0-933087-77-2 $12.95
Jeanne Bryner. *Eclipse: Stories*. 2003 / 0-933087-78-0 $12.95
Richard Hague. *Alive in Hard Times: Poems*. 2003 / 0933087-83-7 $12.00
Paola Corso. *Death by Renaissance: Poems & Photos*. 2004 /
0933087-86-1 $12.00
Jeff Vande Zande. *Emergency Stopping & Other Stories*. 2004
0-933087-87-X $12.95